School D

RUSKIN BOND'S first novel, *The Room on the Roof*, written when he was seventeen, won the John Llewellyn Rhys Memorial Prize in 1957. Since then he has written several novellas (including *Vagrants in the Valley*, *A Flight of Pigeons* and *Delhi is Not Far*), essays, poems and children's books. He has also written over 500 short stories and articles that have appeared in a number of magazines and anthologies. He received the Sahitya Akademi Award in 1993 for *Our Trees Still Grow in Dehra*, a collection of short stories, and the Padma Shri in 1999.

Contents

Miss Babcock's Big Toe

Ruskin Bond

IF TWO PEOPLE ARE THROWN TOGETHER FOR A LONG TIME, THEY can become either close friends or sworn enemies.

Thus it was with Tata and me when we both went down with mumps and had to spend a fortnight together in the school hospital. It wasn't really a hospital – just a five-bed ward in a small cottage on the approach road to our prep school in Chotta Simla. It was supervised by a retired nurse, an elderly matron called Miss Babcock who was all but stone deaf.

Miss Babcock was an able nurse, but she was a fidgety, fussy person, always dashing about from ward to dispensary, to her own room, and as a result the boys called her Miss Shuttlecock. As she couldn't hear us, she didn't mind. But her hearing difficulty did create something of a problem – both for her and for her patients. If someone in the ward felt ill late at night, he had to shout or ring a bell – and she heard neither. So someone had to get up and fetch her.

Miss Babcock devised an ingenious method of waking her in an emergency. She tied a long piece of string to the foot of a sick person's bed; then took the other end of the string to her own room where, upon retiring for the night, she tied it to her big toe.

A vigorous pull on the string from the sick person, and Miss Babcock would be wide awake!

Now, what could be more tempting than this device? The string was tied to the foot of Tata's bed, and he was a restless fellow, always wanting water, always complaining of aches and pains. And sometimes, out of plain mischief, he would give several tugs on that string until Miss Babcock arrived with a pill or a glass of water.

'You'll have my toe off by morning,' she complained. 'You don't have to pull quite so hard.'

And what was worse, when Tata did fall asleep, he snored to high heaven and nothing could wake him! I had to lie awake most of the night, listening to his rhythmic snoring. It was like a trumpet tuning up. Or a bull-frog calling to its mate.

Fortunately, a couple of nights later, we were joined in the ward by Bimal, a friend and fellow 'feather', who had also contracted mumps. One night of Tata's snoring, and Bimal resolved to do something about it.

'Wait until he's fast asleep,' said Bimal, 'and then we'll carry his bed outside and leave him on the veranda.' We did more than that. As Tata commenced his nightly imitation of the all-wind instruments in the London Philharmonic Orchestra, we pushed up his bed as gently as possible and carried it out into the garden, putting it down beneath the nearest pine tree.

'It's healthier outside,' said Bimal, justifying our action. 'All this fresh air should cure him.'

Leaving Tata to serenade the stars, we returned to the ward and enjoyed a good night's sleep. So did Miss Babcock.

In fact, no one slept because we were woken by Miss Babcock running around the ward screaming 'Where's Tata there was no sign.' Instead, a large black-faced langur sat at the foot of the bed, showing us its teeth in a grin of disfavor.

'Tata's gone,' gasped Miss Babcock.

'He must be a sleep-walker too,' said Bimal.

'Maybe the leopard took him,' I said. Just then there was a commotion in the shrubbery at the end of the garden, and shouting 'Help, help!' Tata emerged from the bushes, followed by several lithe, long-tailed langurs, merrily, giving chase. Apparently he'd woken up at the crack of dawn, to find his bed surrounded by a gang of inquisitive simians. They had meant no harm; but Tata had panicked, and made a dash for life and liberty, running into the forest instead of into the cottage. We got Tata and his bed back into the ward, and Miss Babcock took his temperature and gave him a dose of salts. Oddly enough, in all the excitement no one asked how Tata and his bed had travelled in the night. And strange to say, he did not snore the following night, so maybe the pine-scented night air really helped. Needless to say, we soon recovered from the mumps, and Miss Babcock's big toe received a well-deserved rest.

Tom Sawyer

Mark Twain

THERE WAS SOMETHING ABOUT AUNT POLLY'S MANNER WHEN SHE kissed Tom, that swept away his low spirits and made him light-hearted and happy again. He started to school, and had the luck of coming upon Becky Thatcher at the head of Meadow Lane. His mood always determined his manner. Without a moment's hesitation he ran to her and said:

'I acted mighty mean today, Becky, and I'm so sorry. I won't ever, ever do it that way again as long as ever I live – please make up, won't you?'

The girl stopped and looked at him scornfully in the face.

'I'll thank you to keep yourself to yourself, Mr Thomas Sawyer. I'll never speak to you again.'

She tossed her head and passed on. Tom was so stunned that he had not even presence of mind enough to say 'Who cares,

Miss Smarty?' until the right time to say it had gone by. So he said nothing. But he was in a fine rage, nevertheless. He moped into the school-yard wishing she were a boy, and imagining how he would trounce her if she were. He presently encountered her and delivered a stinging remark as he passed. She hurled one in return, and the angry breach was complete. It seemed to Becky, in her hot resentment, that she could hardly wait for school to 'take in', she was so impatient to see Tom flogged for the injured spelling-book. If she had had any lingering notion of exposing Alfred Temple, Tom's offensive fling had driven it entirely away.

Poor girl, she did not know how fast she was nearing trouble herself. The master, Mr Dobbins, had reached middle age with an unsatisfied ambition. The darling of his desires was to be a doctor, but poverty had decreed that he should be nothing higher than a village schoolmaster. Every day he took a mysterious book out of his desk, and absorbed himself in it at times when no classes were reciting. He kept that book under lock and key. There was not an urchin in school but was perishing to have a glimpse of it, but the chance never came. Every boy and girl had a theory about the nature of that book; but no two theories were alike, and there was no way of getting at the facts in the case. Now as Becky was passing by the desk, which stood near the door, she noticed that the key was in the lock! It was a precious moment. She glanced around; found herself alone, and the next instant she had the book in her hands. The title-page – Professor somebody's Anatomy – carried no information to her mind; so she began to turn the leaves. She came at once upon a handsomely engraved and coloured frontispiece – a human figure. At that moment a shadow fell on the page, and Tom Sawyer stepped in at the door and caught a glimpse of the picture. Becky snatched at the book to close it, and had the hard luck to tear the pictured page half down the middle. She thrust the volume into the desk, turned the key, and burst out crying with shame and vexation:

'Tom Sawyer, you are just as mean as you can be, to sneak up on a person and look at what they're looking at.'

'How could I know you are looking at anything?'

'You ought to be ashamed of yourself, Tom Sawyer; you know you're going to tell on me; and, oh, what shall I do, what shall I do? I'll be whipped, and I was never whipped in school.'

Then she stamped her little foot and said:

'Be so mean if you want to! I know something that's going to happen. You just wait, and you'll see! Hateful, hateful, hateful!' – and she flung out of the house with a new explosion of crying.

Tom stood still, rather flustered by this onslaught. Presently he said to himself:

'What a curious kind of a fool a girl is. Never been licked in school! Shucks, what's a licking! That's just like a girl – they're so thin-skinned and chicken-hearted. Well, of course I ain't going to tell old Dobbins on this little fool, because there's other ways of getting even on her that ain't so mean; but what of it? Old Dobbins will ask who it was tore his book. Nobody'll answer. Then he'll do just the way he always does – ask first one and then t'other, and when he comes to the right girl he'll know it, without any telling. Girls' faces always tell on them. They ain't got any backbone. She'll get licked. Well, it's a kind of a tight place for Becky Thatcher, because there ain't any way out of it.' Tom conned the thing a moment longer, and then added: 'All right, though; she'd like to see me in just such a fix -- let her sweat it out!'

Tom joined the mob of skylarking scholars outside. In a few moments the master arrived and school 'took in'. Tom did not feel a strong interest in his studies. Every time he stole a glance at the girls' side of the room, Becky's face troubled him. Considering all things, he did not want to pity her, and yet it was all he could do to help it. He could get up no exultation that was really worth the name. Presently the spelling-book discovery was made, and Tom's mind was entirely full of his own matters for a while after that. Becky roused up from her lethargy of distress, and showed good interest in the proceedings. She did not expect that Tom could get out of his trouble by denying that he spilt the ink on the book himself; and she was right. The denial only seemed to make the thing worse for Tom. Becky supposed she would be glad of that, and she tried to believe she was glad of it, but she found she was not certain. When the worst came to the worst, she had an impulse to get up and tell on Alfred Temple, but she made an effort and forced herself to keep still, because, said she to herself, 'He'll tell about me tearing the picture, sure. I wouldn't say a word, not to save his life!'

Tom took his whipping and went back to his seat not at all broken-hearted, for he thought it was possible that he had unknowingly upset the ink on the spelling-book himself, in some skylarking bout – he had denied it for form's sake and because it was custom, and had stuck to the denial from principle.

A whole hour drifted by; the master sat nodding in his throne; the air was drowsy with the hum of study. By-and-by Mr Dobbins straightened himself up, yawned, then unlocked his desk, and reached for his book, but seemed undecided whether to take it out or leave it. Most of the pupils glanced up languidly, but there were two among them that watched his movements with intent eyes. Mr Dobbins fingered his book absently for a while, then took it out, and settled himself in his chair to read.

Tom shot a glance at Becky. He had seen a hunted and helpless rabbit look as she did, with a gun levelled at its head. Instantly he forgot his quarrel with her. Quick, something must be done! Done in a flash, too! But the very imminence of the emergency paralysed his invention. Good! he had an inspiration! He would run and snatch the book, spring through the door and fly! But his resolution shook for one little instant, and the chance was lost – the master opened the volume. If Tom only had the wasted opportunity back again! Too late; there was no help for Becky now, he said. The next moment the master faced the school. Every eye sank under his gaze; there was that in it which smote even the innocent with fear. There was silence while one might count ten; the master was gathering his wrath. Then he spoke:

'Who tore this book?'

There was not a sound. One could have heard a pin drop. The stillness continued; the master searched face after face for signs of guilt.

'Benjamin Rogers, did you tear this book?'

A denial. Another pause.

'Joseph Harper, did you?'

Another denial. Tom's uneasiness grew more and more intense under the slow torture of these proceedings. The master scanned the ranks of boys, considered a while, then turned to the girls:

'Amy Lawrence?'

A shake of the head.

'Grade Miller?'

The same sign.

'Susan Harper, did you do this?'

Another negative. The next girl was Becky Thatcher. Tom was trembling from head to foot with excitement, and a sense of the hopelessness of the situation.

'Rebecca Thatcher' – (Tom glanced at her face; it was white with terror) – 'did you tear – no, look me in the face' – (her hands rose in appeal) – 'did you tear this book?'

A thought shot like lightning through Tom's brain. He sprang to his feet and shouted:

'I done it!'

The school stared in perplexity at this incredible folly. Tom stood a moment to gather his dismembered faculties; and when he stepped forward to go to his punishment, the surprise, the gratitude, the adoration that shone upon him out of poor Becky's eyes seemed pay enough for a hundred floggings. Inspired by the splendour of his own act, he took without an outcry the most merciless flogging that even Mr Dobbins had ever administered; and also received with indifference the added cruelty of a command to remain two hours after school should be dismissed – for he knew who would wait for him outside till his captivity was done, and not count the tedious time as loss either.

Tom went to bed that night planning vengeance against Alfred Temple; for with shame and repentance Becky had told him all, not forgetting her own treachery; but even the longing for vengeance had to give way soon to pleasanter musings, and he fell asleep at last with Becky's latest words lingering dreamily in his ear:

'Tom, how could you be so noble!'

David Copperfield
Fights the Canterbury 'Lamb'

Charles Dickens

As every reader knows, Charles Dickens's David Copperfield, apart from being his best if not most popular novel, is largely the story of the author's own boyhood. David was first sent to a bad school (Creakle's), where he and the other boys were ill-used. But at the age of twelve he was, through the knavery of his guardian, put to work in a factory; whence he escaped – tramping from London to Dover, where he found happiness with a kind aunt who adopted him. She sent him to the school here described, which the present editor believes to be King's School, Canterbury. David boards with Mr Wickfield, the aunt's solicitor and friend, whose clerk is the repulsive Uriah Heep.

NEXT MORNING, AFTER BREAKFAST, I ENTERED ON SCHOOL LIFE again. I went, accompanied by Mr Wickfield, to the scene of my future studies – a grave building in a courtyard, with a learned air about it that seemed very well suited to the stray rooks and jackdaws who came down from the Cathedral towers to walk with a clerkly bearing on the grassplot – and was introduced to my new master, Doctor Strong.

Doctor Strong looked almost as rusty, to my thinking, as the tall iron rails and gates outside the house; and almost as stiff and heavy as the great stone urns that flanked them, and were set up, on the top of the red-brick wall, at regular distances all round the court, like sublimated skittles, for time to play at. He was in his library (I mean Doctor Strong was), with his clothes not particularly well brushed, and his hair not particularly well combed; his knee-smalls unbraced; his long black gaiters unbuttoned; and his shoes yawning like two caverns on the hearth-rug. Turning upon me a lustreless eye, that reminded me of a long-forgotten blind old horse who once used to crop the grass; and tumble over the graves, in Blunderstone churchyard, he said he was glad to see me: and then he gave me his hand; which I didn't know what to do with, as it did nothing for itself. . . .

The schoolroom was a pretty large hall, on the quietest side of the house, confronted by the stately stare of some half-dozen of the great urns, and commanding a peep of an old secluded garden belonging to the Doctor, where the peaches were ripening on the sunny south wall. There were two great aloes, in tubs, on the turf outside the windows; the broad hard leaves of which plant (looking as if they were made of painted tin) have ever since, by association, been symbolical to me of silence and retirement. About five-and-twenty boys were studiously engaged at their books when we went in, but they rose to give the Doctor good morning, and remained standing when they saw Mr Wickfield and me.

'A new boy, young gentlemen,' said the Doctor; 'Trotwood Copperfield.'

One Adams, who was the head-boy, then stepped out of his place and welcomed me. He looked like a young clergyman, in his white cravat, but he was very affable and good-humoured; and he showed me my place, and presented me to the masters, in a gentlemanly way that would have put me at my ease, if anything could.

It seemed to me so long, however, since I had been among such boys, or among any companions of my own age, except Mick Walker and Mealy Potatoes, that I felt as strange as ever I have done in all my life. I was so conscious of having passed through scenes of which they could have no knowledge, and of having acquired experiences foreign to my age, appearance, and condition as one of them, that I half believed it was an imposture to come there as an ordinary little schoolboy.

Seeing a light in the little round office, and immediately feeling myself attracted towards Uriah Heep, who had a sort of fascination for me, I went in there instead. I found Uriah reading a great fat book, with such demonstrative attention, that his lank forefinger followed up every line as he read, and made clammy tracks along the page (or so I fully believed) like a snail.

'You are working late tonight, Uriah,' I say.

'Yes, Master Copperfield,' says Uriah.

As I was getting on the stool opposite, to talk to him more conveniently, I observed that he had not such a thing as a smile about him, and that he could only widen his mouth and make two hard creases down his cheeks, one on each side, to stand for one.

'I am not doing office-work, Master Copperfield,' said Uriah.

'What work, then?' I asked.

'I am improving my legal knowledge, Master Copperfield,' said Uriah. 'I am going through Tidd's Practice. Oh, what a writer Mr Tidd is, Master Copperfield!'

My stool was such a tower of observation, that as I watched him reading on again, after this rapturous exclamation, and following up the lines with his forefinger, I observed that his nostrils, which were thin and pointed, with sharp dints in them, had a singular and most uncomfortable way of expanding and contracting themselves; that they seemed to twinkle instead of his eyes, which hardly ever twinkled at all.

'I suppose you are quite a great lawyer?' I said, after looking at him for some time.

'Me, Master Copperfield?' said Uriah. 'Oh, no! I'm a very humble person.'

It was no fancy of mine about his hands, I observed; for he frequently grounded the palms against each other as if to squeeze them dry and warm, besides often wiping them, in a stealthy way, on his pocket-handkerchief.

'I am well aware that I am the humblest person going,' said Uriah Heep, modestly; 'let the other be where he may. My mother is likewise a very humble person. We live in a humble abode, Master Copperfield, but have much to be thankful for. My father's former calling was humble. He was a sexton."

'What is he now?' I asked.

'He is a partaker of glory at present, Master Copperfield,' said Uriah Heep. 'But we have much to be thankful for. How much have I to be thankful for in living with Mr Wickfield!'

I asked Uriah if he had been with Mr Wickfield long?

'I have been with him going on four year, Master Copperfield,' said Uriah; shutting up his book, after carefully marking the place where he had left off. 'Since a year after my father's death. How much have I to be thankful for, in that! How much have I to be thankful for, in Mr Wickfield's kind intention to give me my articles, which would otherwise not lay within the humble means of mother and self!"

'Then, when your articled time is over, you'll be a regular lawyer, I suppose?' I said.

'With the blessing of Providence, Master Copperfield,' returned Uriah.

'Perhaps you'll be a partner in Mr Wickfield's business, one of these days,' I said, to make myself agreeable; 'and it will be Wickfield and Heep, or Heep late Wickfield.'

'Oh, no, Master Copperfield,' returned Uriah, shaking his head, 'I am much too humble for that!'

He certainly did look uncommonly like the carved face on the beam outside my window, as he sat, in his humility, eyeing me sideways, with his mouth widened, and the creases in his cheeks.

'Mr Wickfield is a most excellent man, Master Copper-field,' said Uriah. 'If you have known him long, you, know it, I am sure, much better than I can inform you.'

I replied that I was certain he was; but that I had not known him long myself, though he was a friend of my aunt's.

'Oh, indeed, Master Copperfield,' said Uriah. 'Your aunt is a sweet lady, Master Copperfield!'

He had a way of writhing when he wanted to express enthusiasm, which was very ugly; and which diverted my attention from the compliment he had paid my relation, to the snaky twistings of his throat and body.

'A sweet lady, Master Copperfield!' said Uriah Heep. 'She has a great admiration for Miss Agnes, Master Copperfield, I believe?'

I said, 'Yes,' boldly; not that I knew anything about it, Heaven forgive me!

'I hope you have, too, Master Copperfield,' said Uriah. 'But I am sure you must have.'

'Everybody must have,' I returned.

'Oh, thank you, Master Copperfield,' said Uriah Heep, 'for that remark! It is so true! Humble as I am, I know it is so true! Oh, thank you, Master Copperfield!'

He writhed himself quite off his stool in the excitement of his feelings, and, being off, began to make arrangements for going home.

'Mother will be expecting me,' he said, referring to a pale, inexpressive-faced watch in his pocket, 'and getting uneasy; for though we are very humble, Master Copperfield, we are much attached to one another. If you would come and see us, any afternoon, and take a cup of tea at our lowly dwelling, mother would be as proud of your company as I should be.'

I said I should be glad to come.

'Thank you, Master Copperfield,' returned Uriah, putting his book away upon the shelf. 'I suppose you stop here, some time, Master Copperfield?'

I said I was going to be brought up there, I believed, as long as I remained at school.

'Oh, indeed!' exclaimed Uriah. 'I should think you would come into the business at last, Master Copperfield!' I protested that I had no views of that sort, and that no such scheme was entertained in my behalf by anybody; but Uriah insisted on blandly replying to all my assurances, 'Oh, yes, Master Copperfield, I should think you would, indeed!' and, 'Oh, indeed, Master Copperfield, I should think you would, certainly!' over and over again. Being, at last, ready to leave the office for the night, he asked me if it would suit my convenience to have the light put out; and on my answering 'Yes,' instantly extinguished it. After shaking hands with me – his hand felt like a fish, in the dark – he opened the door into the street a very little, and crept out, and shut it, leaving me to grope my way back into the house: which cost me some trouble and a fall over his stool.

My schooldays! The silent gliding on of my existence – the unseen, unfelt progress of my life – from childhood up to youth! Let me think, as I look back upon that flowing water, now a dry channel overgrown with leaves, whether there are any marks along its course, by which I can remember how it ran.

A moment, and I occupy my place in the Cathedral, where we all went together, every Sunday morning, assembling first at school for that purpose. The earthy smell, the sunless air, the sensation of the world being shut out, the resounding of the organ through the black and white arched galleries and aisles, are wings that take me back, and hold me hovering above those days, in a half-sleeping and half-waking dream.

I am not the last boy in the school. I have risen, in a few months, over several heads. But the first boy seems to me a mighty creature, dwelling afar off, whose giddy height is unattainable. Agnes says 'No,' but I say 'Yes,' and tell her that she little thinks what stores of knowledge have been mastered by the wonderful Being, at whose place she thinks I, even I, weak aspirant, may arrive in time. He is not my private friend and public patron, as Steerforth was; but I hold him in a reverential respect. I chiefly wonder what he'll be, when he leaves Doctor Strong's, and what mankind will do to maintain any place against him.

But who is this that breaks upon me? This is Miss Shepherd, whom I love.

Miss Shepherd is a boarder at the Misses Nettingalls' establishment. I adore Miss Shepherd. She is a little girl, in a spencer, with a round face and curly flaxen hair. The Misses Nettingalls' young ladies come to the Cathedral too. I cannot look upon my book, for I must look upon Miss Shepherd. When the choristers chant, I hear Miss Shepherd. In the service, I mentally insert Miss Shepherd's name – I put her in among the Royal Family. At home, in my own room, I am sometimes moved to cry out, 'Oh, Miss Shepherd!' in a transport of love.

For some time, I am doubtful of Miss Shepherd's feelings, but, at length, fate being propitious, we meet at the dancing school. I have Miss Shepherd for my partner. I touch Miss Shepherd's glove, and feel a thrill go up the right arm of my jacket, and come out at my hair. I say nothing tender to Miss Shepherd, but we understand each other. Miss Shepherd and myself live but to be united.

Why do I secretly give Miss Shepherd twelve Brazil nuts for a present, I wonder? They are not expressive of affection, they are difficult to pack into a parcel of any regular shape, they are hard to crack, even in room-doors, and they are oily when cracked; yet I feel that they are appropriate to Miss Shepherd. Soft, seedy biscuits, also, I bestow upon Miss Shepherd; and oranges innumerable. Once, I kiss Miss Shepherd in the cloakroom. Ecstasy! What are my agony and indignation next day, when I hear a flying rumour that the Misses Nettingall has stood Miss Shepherd in the stocks for turning in her toes!

Miss Shepherd being the one pervading theme and vision of my life, how do I ever come to break with her? I can't conceive. And yet a coolness grows between Miss Shepherd and myself. Whispers reach me of Miss Shepherd having said she wished I wouldn't stare so, and having avowed a preference for Master Jones – for Jones! A boy of no merit whatever! The gulf between me and Miss Shepherd widens. At last, one day, I meet the Misses Nettingalls' establishment out walking. Miss Shepherd makes a face as she goes by, and laughs to her companion. All is over. The devotion of a life – it seems a life, it is all the same – is at an end; Miss Shepherd comes out of the morning service, and the Royal Family knows her no more.

I am higher in the school, and no one breaks my peace. I am not at all polite, now, to the Misses Nettingalls' young ladies, and shouldn't dote on any of them, if they were twice as many and twenty times as beautiful. I think the dancing school a tiresome affair, and wonder why the girls can't dance by themselves and leave us alone. I am growing great in Latin verses, and neglect the laces of my boots. Doctor Strong refers to me in public as a promising young scholar. Mr Dick is wild with joy, and my aunt remits me a guinea by the next post.

The shade of a young butcher rises, like the apparition of an armed head in Macbeth. Who is this young butcher? He is the terror of the youth of Canterbury. There is a vague belief abroad, that the beef suet with which he anoints his hair gives him unnatural strength, and that he is a match for a man. He is a broad-faced, bull-necked young butcher, with rough red cheeks, an ill-conditioned mind, and an injurious tongue. His main use of this tongue is to disparage Doctor Strong's young gentlemen. He says, publicly, that if they want anything he'll give it to 'em.

le names individuals among them (myself included), whom he
ould undertake to settle with one hand, and the other tied behind
im. He waylays the smaller boys to punch their unprotected
leads, and calls challenges after me in the open streets. For these
ufficient reasons I resolve to fight the butcher.

It is a summer evening, down in a green hollow, at the corner
f a wall. I meet the butcher by appointment. I am attended by
select body of our boys; the butcher, by two other butchers,
young publican, and a sweep. The preliminaries are adjusted,
nd the butcher and myself stand face to face. In a moment, the
utcher lights ten thousand candles out of my left eyebrow. In
nother moment, I don't know where the wall is, or where I am,
r where anybody is. I hardly know which is myself and which
ne butcher, we are always in such a tangle and tussle, knocking
bout upon the trodden grass. Sometimes I see the butcher,
loody but confident; sometimes I see nothing, and sit gasping
n my second's knee; sometimes I go in at the butcher madly,
nd cut my knuckles open against his face, without appearing
o discompose him at all. At last I awake, very queer about the
ead, as from a giddy sleep, and see the butcher walking off,
ongratulated by the two other butchers and the sweep and
ublican, and putting on his coat as he goes; from which I augur,
astly, that the victory is his.

I am taken home in a sad plight, and I have beef-steaks put
o my eyes, and am rubbed with vinegar and brandy, and find
great white puffy place bursting out on my upper lip, which
vells immoderately. For three or four days I remain at home, a
ery ill-looking subject, with a green shade over my eyes; and I
ould be very dull, but that Agnes is a sister to me, and condoles
ith me, and reads to me, and makes the time light and happy.

Agnes has my confidence completely, always; I tell her all abou
the butcher, and the wrongs he has heaped upon me; and she
thinks I couldn't have done otherwise than fight the butcher, while
she shrinks and trembles at my having fought him.

Time has stolen on unobserved, for Adams is not the head
boy in the days that are come now, nor has he been this many
and many a day. Adams has left the school so long, that when
he comes back, on a visit to Doctor Strong, there are not many
there, besides myself, who know him. Adams is going to be
called to the bar almost directly, and is to be an advocate, and to
wear a wig. I am surprised to find him a meeker man than I had
thought, and less imposing in appearance. He has not staggered
the world yet, either; for it goes on (as well as I can make out)
pretty much the same as if he had never joined it.

A blank through which the warriors of poetry and history
march on in stately hosts that seem to have no end -- and what
comes next! I am the head-boy now; and look down on the line of
boys below me, with a condescending interest in such of them as
bring to my mind the boy I was myself, when I first came there.
That little fellow seems to be no part of me; I remember him
as something left behind upon the road of life -- as something I
have passed, rather than have actually been -- and almost think
of him as of someone else.

Charles Dickens: David Copperfield (185

Little Jack

Anton Chekhov

This touching story illustrates the great writer's ability to inhabit his characters and identify with them. As a result, Little Jack continues to exist beyond the confines of the story. . . .

JACK JUKOFF WAS A LITTLE BOY OF NINE WHO, THREE MONTHS AGO, had been apprenticed to Aliakin, the shoemaker. On Christmas Eve he did not go to bed. He waited until his master and the foreman had gone out to church, and then fetched a bottle of ink and a rusty pen from his master's cupboard, spread out a crumpled sheet of paper before him, and began to write. Before he had formed the first letter he had more than once looked fearfully round at the door, glanced at the icon, on each side of which were ranged shelves laden with boot-lasts, and sighed deeply. The paper lay spread on the bench, and before it knelt Little Jack.

Dear Grandpapa – Constantine Makaritch (he wrote), I am writing you a letter. I wish you a merry Christmas and I hope God will give you all sorts of good things. I have no papa or mamma, and you are all I have.

Little Jack turned his eyes to the dark window, on which shone the reflection of the candle, and vividly pictured to himself his grandfather, Constantine Makaritch: a small, thin, but extraordinarily active old man of sixty-five, with bleary eyes and a perpetually smiling face; by day sleeping in the kitchen or teasing the cook; by night, muffled in a huge sheepskin coat, walking about the garden beating his watchman's rattle. Behind him, hanging their heads, pace the dogs Kashtanka and The Eel, so called because he is black and his body is long like a weasel's. The Eel is uncommonly respectful and affectionate; he gazes with impartial fondness upon strangers and friends alike; but his credit, in spite of this, is bad. Beneath the disguise of a humble and deferential manner he conceals the most Jesuitical perfidy. Nobody knows better than he how to steal up and grab you by the leg, how to make his way into the ice-house, or filch a hen from a peasant. His hind legs have been broken more than once; twice he has been hung, and every week he is thrashed within an inch of his life; but he always recovers.

At this moment, no doubt, grandfather is standing at the gate blinking at the glowing red windows of the village church, stamping his felt boots, and teasing the servants. His rattle hangs at his belt. He beats his arms and hugs himself with cold, and giggling after the manner of old men, pinches first the maid, then the cook.

'Let's have some snuff!' he says, handing the women his snuff-box.

The women take snuff and sneeze. Grandfather goes off into indescribable ecstasies, breaks into shouts of laughter, and cries:

'Wipe it off! It's freezing on!'

Then they give the dogs snuff. Kashtanka sneezes and wrinkles her nose; her feelings are hurt, and she walks away. The Eel refrains from sneezing out of respect and wags his tail. The weather is glorious. The night is dark, but the whole village is visible; the white roofs, the columns of smoke rising from the chimneys, the trees, silvery with frost, and the snowdrifts. The sky is strewn with gaily twinkling stars, and the milky way is as bright as if it had been washed and scrubbed with snow for the holiday.

Little Jack sighed, dipped his pen in the ink, and went on:

I had a dragging yesterday. My master dragged me into the yard by my hair and beat me with a stirrup because I went to sleep without meaning to while I was rocking the baby. Last week my mistress told me to clean some herrings, and I began cleaning one from the tail, and she took it and poked its head into my face. The foreman laughs at me and sends me for vodka, makes me steal the cucumbers, and then my master beats me with whatever comes handy. And I have nothing to eat. I get bread in the morning, and porridge for dinner, and bread for supper. My master and mistress drink up all the tea and the soup. And they make me sleep in the hall, and when the baby cries I don't sleep at all because I have to rock the cradle. Dear grandpa, please take me away from here, home to the village. I can't stand it. I beg you on my knees; I will pray to God for you all my life. Take me away from here, or else I shall die. . . .

Little Jack's mouth twisted; he rubbed his eyes with a grimy fist and cried:

I will grind your tobacco for you, he continued, and pray to God for you; and if I don't you can kill me like Sidoroff's goat. And if you think I ought to work I can ask the steward please to let me take the boots, or I can do the ploughing in place of Teddy. Dear Grandpa, I can't stand it; I shall die. I wanted to run away to the village on foot, but I haven't any boots, and it is so cold. And when I am big I will always take care of you and not allow anyone to hurt you at all, and when you die I will pray to God for you as I do for my mother, Pelagea.

Moscow is a big city. All the houses are manor houses, and there are lots of horses, but no sheep, and the dogs are not fierce. The children don't carry stars,[1] and they don't let anyone sing in church, and in one store I saw in the window how they were selling fish-hooks with the lines on them, and there was a fish on every hook, and the hooks were very large and one held a sturgeon that weighed forty pounds. I saw a store where they sell all kinds of guns just like our master's guns; some cost a hundred roubles. But at the butcher's there are grouse and partridges and hares; but the butcher won't tell where they were killed.

Dear Grandpa, when they have the Christmas tree at the big house, keep some gold nuts for me and put them away in the green chest. Ask Miss Olga for them and say they are for Little Jack.

---

[1] A Russian peasant custom at Christmas time.

Little Jack heaved a shuddering sigh and stared at the window again. He remembered how his grandfather used to go to the forest for the Christmas tree, and take his grandchild with him. Those were jolly days. Grandfather wheezed and grunted, and the snow wheezed and grunted, and Little Jack wheezed and grunted in sympathy. Before cutting down the tree grandfather would finish smoking his pipe and slowly take snuff, laughing all the time at little, shivering Jacky. The young fir trees, muffled in snow, stood immovable and wondered: 'Which of us is going to die?' Hares flew like arrows across the snow, and grandfather could never help crying: 'Hold on! Hold on! Hold on! Oh, the bobtailed devil!'

Then grandfather would drag the fallen fir tree up to the big house, and there they would all set to work trimming it. The busiest of all was Miss Olga, Jack's favourite. While Jack's mother, Pelagea, was still alive and a housemaid at the big house, Miss Olga used to give Little Jack candy, and because she had nothing better to do had taught him to read and write and to count up to a hundred, and even to dance the quadrille.

When Pelagea died the little orphan was banished to the kitchen, where his grandfather was, and from there he was sent to Moscow, to Aliakin, the shoemaker.

Do come, dear grandpapa (Little Jack went on). Please come; I beg you for Christ's sake to come and take me away. Have pity on your poor little orphan, because everyone scolds me, and I'm so hungry, and it's so lonely – I can't tell you how lonely it is. I cry all day long. And the other day my master hit me on the head with a boot tree, so that I fell down and almost didn't come to again.

And give my love to Nelly and one-eyed Gregory and to the coachman, and don't let anyone use my accordion.

Your grandson,
John Jukoff

Dear Grandpapa, do come.

Little Jack folded the paper in four and put it in an envelope which he had bought that evening for one copeck. He reflected an instant, then dipped his pen in the ink and wrote the address:

To my Grandpapa in the Village.

Then he scratched his head, thought a moment, and added:

Constantine Makaritch.

Delighted to have finished his letter without interruption, he put on his cap and, without waiting to throw his little overcoat over his shoulders, ran out into the street in his shirt.

The butcher, whom he had asked the evening before, had told him that one drops letters into the mail-boxes, and that from there they are carried all over the world in mail wagons with ringing bells, driven by drivers who are drunk. Little Jack ran to the nearest mailbox and dropped his letter in the opening.

An hour later he was sound asleep, lulled by the sweetest hope. He dreamed; he saw a stove. On the stove sat his grandfather swinging his bare legs and reading his letter to the cook. Near the stove walked The Eel, wagging his tail.

The Baker's Boy

Samuel Smiles

Robert Dick (1811–1866) was a native of Tullibody, in Clackmannanshire, who became a baker, living in turn in Leith, Glasgow and Greenock, and finally at Thurso. He devoted his spare time to the study of geology and botany, and was inspired by Hugh Miller's Old Red Sandstone, published in 1841. He was soon in communication with Miller, and sent him many rare geological specimens collected in his own district. In this way he made many valuable contributions to the growth of geological knowledge.

ROBERT DICK WAS APPRENTICED TO MR AIKMAN, A BAKER IN Tullibody, when he was thirteen years old. Mr Aikman had a large business, and supplied bread to people in the neighbouring villages as far as the Bridge of Allan.

The life of a baker is by no means interesting. One day is like another. The baker is up in the morning at three or four.

The oven fire is kindled first. The flour is mixed with yeast and salt and water, laboriously kneaded together. The sponge is then set in some warm place. The dough begins to rise. After mingling with more flour, and thorough kneading, the mass is weighed into lumps of the proper size, which are shaped into loaves and 'bricks', or into 'baps', penny and half-penny. This is the batch, which, after a short time, is placed in the oven until it is properly baked and ready to be taken out. The bread is then sold or delivered to the customers. When delivered out of doors, the bread is placed on a flat baker's basket, and carried on the head from place to place.

Robert Dick got up first and kindled the fire, so as to heat the oven preparatory to the batch being put in. His nephew, Mr Alexander of Dunfermline, says, 'He got up at three in the morning, and worked and drudged until seven and eight, and sometimes nine o'clock at night.'

As he grew older, and was strong enough to carry the basket on his head, he was sent about to deliver the bread in the neighbouring villages. He was sent to Menstrie, to Lipney on the Ochils, to Blairlogie at the foot of Dunmyat, and farther westward to the Bridge of Allan, about six miles from Tullibody.

The afternoons on which he delivered the bread were a great pleasure to Dick. He had an opportunity for observing nature, which had charms for him in all its moods. When he went up the hills to Lipney, he wandered on his return through Menstrie Glen. He watched the growth of the plants. He knew them individually, one from the other. He began to detect the differences between them, though he then knew little about orders, classes, and genera. When the hazel-nuts were ripe he gathered them and brought loads of them home, for the enjoyment of his master's brains. They all had a great love for the prentice Robert.

He must also, in course of time, have obtained some special acquaintance with botany. At all events, he inquired, many years after, about some particular plants which he had observed during his residence at Dam's Burn and Tullibody. 'Send me,' he said to his eldest sister, 'a twig with the blossom and some leaves, from the Tron Tree in Tullibody.' The Tron Tree is a lime tree standing nearly opposite the house in which Robert was born.

'Send me also,' he said, 'a specimen of the wild geranium, which you will find on the old road close by the foot of the hills between Menstrie and Alva. I also want a water-plant (describing it) which grows in the river Devon.' The two former were sent to him, but the water-plant could not be found.

Robert's apprenticeship lasted for three years and a half. He got no wages – only his meals and his bed. He occupied a small room over the bakehouse. His father had still to clothe him, and his washing was done at home. On Saturdays he went with his 'duds' to Dam's Burn. But either soap was scarce, or good-will was wanting. His step-mother would not give him clean stockings except once a fortnight. His sister Agnes used to accompany him home to Tullibody in the evening, and at the Aikmans' door she exchanged stockings with him, promising to have his own well darned and washed by the following Sunday.

The day of rest was a day of pleasure to him. He did not care to stay within doors. He had shoes now, and could wander up the hills to the top of Dunmyat or Bencleuch, and see the glorious prospect of the country below; the windings of the Devon, the windings of the Forth, and the country far away, from the castle of Stirling on the one hand to the castle of Edinburgh on the other.

Dick continued to be a great reader. He read every book that he could lay his hands on. Popular books were not so common then as they are now. But he contrived to borrow some volumes of the old *Edinburgh Encyclopaedia,* and this gave him an insight into science. It helped him in his knowledge of botany. He could now find out for himself the names of the plants; and he even began to make a collection. It could only have been a small one, for his time was principally occupied by labour. Yet, with a thirst for knowledge, and a determination to obtain it, a great deal may be accomplished in even the humblest station.

In 1826, Mr Dick was advanced to the office of supervisor of excise, and removed to Thurso. Robert was then left to himself in Tullibody. He had still two years more to serve. One day followed another in the usual round of daily toil. The toil was, however, mingled with pleasure, and he walked through the country with his bread basket, and watched Nature with ever-increasing delight.

He made no acquaintances. The Aikmans say that he was very kind to his master's children – that he was constantly bringing them flowers from the fields, or nuts from the glens, or anything curious or interesting which he had picked up in the course of his journeys. He occupied a little of his time in bird-stuffing. He stuffed a hare, which he called 'a tinkler's lion.' It needs scarcely be said that the children were very fond of their father's prentice.

At length his time was out. He was only seventeen. But he had to leave Tullibody, and try to find work as a journeyman. He bundled up his clothes and set out for Alloa, where he caught the boat for Leith. He never saw Tullibody again, though he long remembered it. His father and mother were buried in the churchyard there; and he could not help having a longing affection for the place. But he could never spare money enough to revisit the place of his birth.

Long after, when writing to his brother-in-law, he said, 'And ye have been up to Alloa. Well, I do believe that is a bonnie country, altho' I fancy it is not in any sense the poor man's country. Nothing but men of money there; though feint a hair did I care for their grandeur while I lived there. The hills and woods, and freedom to run upon them and through them, was all I cared about.

What though, like commoners of air,
We wander out we know not where,
But either house or hall?
Yet Nature's charms, the hills and woods,
The sweeping vales, and foaming floods
Are free alike to all.

I daresay I might pick up a plant or a stone with very different feelings from those I felt in the days of old. But let them go! There is no use in repining.'

Again, when writing to a fellow botanist, who doubted whether *Digitalis purpurea* was a native of Caithness, he said, 'I have seen more of the plant in Caithness than I ever saw about Stirling, Alloa, or on the Ochil hills -- more than I ever saw in the woods of Tullibody.'

Robert Dick found a journeyman's situation at Leith, where he remained for six months. His life there was composed of the usual round of getting up early in the morning, kneading, baking, and going about the streets with his basket on his head, delivering bread to the customers. It was a lonely life; and the more lonely, as he was far away from Nature and the hills that he loved.

From Leith he went to Glasgow, and afterwards to Greenock. He was a journeyman baker for about three years. His wages were small; his labour was heavy; and he did not find that he was making much progress. He continued to correspond with his father, and told him of his position. The father said, 'Come to Thurso, and set up a baker's shop here.' There were then only three bakers' shops in the whole county of Caithness – one at Thurso, one at Castleton, and another at Wick.

In that remote district 'baker's bread' had scarcely come into fashion. The people there lived chiefly on oatmeal and bere[2] – oatmeal porridge and cakes, and barley bannocks, with plenty of milk. Upon this fare men and women grew up strong and healthy. Many of them only got a baker's loaf for 'the Sabbath'.

Robert Dick took his father's advice. He went almost to the world's end to set up his trade. He arrived at Thurso in the summer of 1830, when he was about twenty years old. A shop was taken in Wilson's Lane, nearly opposite his father's house. An oven had to be added to the premises before the business could be begun; and in the meantime Robert surveyed the shore along Thurso Bay.

Thurso is within sight of Orkney, the Ultima Thule of the Romans. It is the northernmost town in Great Britain. John o Groat's – the Land's End of Scotland – is farther to the east. It consists of only a few green mounds, indicating where John o Groat's House once stood.

Thurso is situated at the southern end of Thurso Bay, at the mouth of the Thurso river – the most productive salmon river in Scotland. The fish, after feeding and cleaning themselves in

---

[2]Bere or bar (Norwegian), a commoner kind of barley.

the Pentland Firth, make for the fresh water. The first river they come to is the Thurso, up which they swim in droves.

Thurso Bay, whether in fair or foul weather, is a grand sight. On the eastern side, the upright cliffs of Dunnet Head run far to the northward, forming the most northerly point of the Scottish mainland. On the west, a high crest of land juts out into the sea, forming at its extremity the bold precipitous rocks of Holborn Head. Looking out of the Bay you see the Orkney Islands in the distance, the Old Man of Hoy standing up at its western promontory. At sunset the light glints along the island, showing the bold prominences and depressions in the red sandstone cliffs. Out into the ocean the distant sails of passing ships are seen against the sky, white as a gull's wing.

The long swelling waves of the Atlantic come rolling in upon the beach. The noise of their breaking in stormy weather is like thunder. From Thurso they are seen dashing over the Holborn Head, though some two hundred feet high; and the cliffs beyond Dunnet Bay are hid in spray.

Robert Dick was delighted with the sea in all its aspects. The sea opens many a mind. The sea is the most wonderful thing a child can see; and it long continues to fill the thoughtful mind with astonishment. The seashore on the western coast is full of strange sights. There is nothing but sea between Thurso and the coasts of Labrador.

The wash of the ocean comes by the Gulf Stream round the western coasts of Scotland, and along the northern coasts of Norway. Hence, the bits of driftwood, the tropical seaweed, and the tropical nuts, thrown upon the shore at Thurso.

In the same way, bits of mahogany are sometimes carried by the ocean current from Honduras or the Bay of Mexico, and thrown upon the shore on the northernmost coasts of Norway. One evening, while walking along the beach near Thurso, Robert Dick took up a singular-looking nut, which he examined. He remarked to the friend who accompanied him, 'That has been brought by the ocean current and the prevailing winds all the way from one of the West Indian Islands. How strange that we should find it here!'

Robert Dick always admired the magnificent sea pictures of Thurso Bay – its waves that gently rocked or wildly raged. He enjoyed the salt-laden breath of the sea wind; and even the cries of the sea birds. Here is his description of the sea-mew: 'Ha ga tirwa!' How strange and uncouth! How very unnatural the cry seemed. It was only the cry of a sea bird. It was within the sight of the ocean. There had been a storm. It was over, but the waves in long rolling breakers dashed themselves in a rage on the sandy shore, and then were quiet. But quiet only for the moment. 'Ha ga tirwa!' Restless and unwearied, another and another long wave followed and burst into spray. And thus it has ever been 'since evening was, and morning was.' It was then evening, the stars began to twinkle; and after a little the full moon rose. But still 'Ha ga tirwa!'

Robert Dick, Baker and Botanist
Samuel Smiles

The Sea in the Bottle

Lionel Seepaul

From Trinidad and Tobago comes the entertaining story of a boy who was a little too smart for his own good . . .
'I held my breath. Did he suspect me?'

WHEN MR CLAYTON, MY NEIGHBOUR WHO SOLD FRUITS FOR A living, gave me a penny a week to watch over his orchard, little did he suspect me. As far as he knew I was the best boy in the village. Promptly and regularly I went to the village school. On Sundays I seldom missed Sunday school. Before church began, I would ring the church bell which could be heard for miles around Waterloo village.

Afterwards I did errands for the villagers. For Widow Critchlow I fetched a bucket of water when her arms ached. And for blind Mr Lomas I brought back in the brown paper bag three loaves of hot bread from the village baker, and the daily newspaper which I read to him at a penny a week.

One day Mr Clayton said to my mother: 'Dis boy is like a young Samuel, and gwine be a preacher one day. Mark my word. He honest and does tell the whole truth. And as from today, he will watch over my garden like Adam. And I will give him a whole penny for the whole week till school holidays end.'

My mother bowed low and raised the broom ever grateful.

'I so thankful, neighbour Clayton. Sunshine not roaming about with them bad boys stoning the dogs, and thiefing up you pineapple and soursop and sapodillas.'

'I done try everything to stop them from thiefing mey fruits. I get a bad dog, but even that dog eat mey food and run away. I sprinkle broken bottles around the garden but is only I who getting mey own foot cut up. Madam, if them boys don't stop robbing me of my honest living I go just have to try the one last thing. . . .'

My mother dropped her broom.

'Not the sea-in-the-bottle curse? O Lord, neighbour Clayton, please don't put that magic spell on none of them bad boys. Take out you belt, and swell up they skin blue-black, but don't put that lifelong curse on them. Now that my Sunshine is your watchman there is no need to put that curse on nobody.'

Everyday now I watched the garden as Mr Clayton rode off to sell mangoes, oranges, star-apples, and chataigne, a small black nut, loaded in the wooden box chained to the back of his Raleigh bicycle.

That weekend I asked my mother what was this sea-in-the-bottle fairy tale.

'You young people does make a joke of everything we big people knows is true. That same curse is what kill Widow Critchlow onliest son. The boy thief the Shango preacher breadfruit. And preacher Lucas put the sea-in-the-bottle curse on the poor widow son.'

So loudly I laughed that my mother struck me with the broom.

'You think is "nancy story – fairy tale," eh?'

Coughing, my eyes were filled with tears from laughing.

Daily, from my window I watched the backyard – crowded with guavas, cashew nuts, plums, coconuts, and a banana tree with a large bunch of bananas.

'Boy, see that bunch of bananas. Guard it as the apple of you eyes,' Mr Clayton repeated as he swung his leg high over the saddle, clinging the bell, and shouting as he rode through the village: 'Fruits, fresh fresh fruits! Two for the price of one.'

As soon as his voice died away, I leaped over the galvanised fence between his house and ours, scrambled up the plum tree, and filled my pockets. Behind his pigsty was a pepper tree with peppers thick like my little finger. In a spoon of salt I crushed the pepper with each plum which I sucked dry and pelted the plum-seed as humming birds pecking at the red rosy cashew, a longish meaty fruit with a light green nut that hung from thin crooked branches.

That cashew tree was my next target.

Much too tired to ever notice any plum missing, Mr Clayton gave me the penny which I dropped into my Ovaltine bank under my bed. Soon I would be able to buy the Parker fountain pen from Chin Lee, the Chinese shopkeeper. For a long time now I had been dropping pennies earned from errands, including the extra penny for guarding the banana tree.

But one day stepping on a plum-seed, my neighbour shouted out: 'Sunshine boy, what kind of watchman you is? It look like

I not going to pay you no penny. Why for you letting them bad boys thief mey plums and mey cashew nuts! I warning I going to put the sea-in-the-bottle curse on they head.'

I was ready with an answer for the silly old man.

'Is not no boy what stealing you nice sweet plums, Mr Clayton. I see with my two eyes those black ugly birds picking the plums. Don't worry. I have my slinging-shot ready and a pocket of small pebbles for them thiefing birds.'

'All right boy, I believes you. I going to sell mey fruits again. But here is another extra penny. Please keep you two eyes on that bunch of bananas. I getting three whole penny for each banana.'

These extra pennies were filling up my Ovaltine bank. Soon I would be able to buy myself a real pen instead of the twig I sharpened and heated into a hard point, which I dipped in the small jar of ink squeezed from black berries growing on vines along the fence.

No sooner had he gone than I leaped over the fence, and with my pocketknife cut a yellowish banana from the underside of the greenish bunch.

'Ha, ha' I laughed the next day. 'Mr Clayton blind like a bat. He can't see behind the bunch.'

And, the next day I stole my second banana.

On the third day, Mr Clayton did not go to sell fruits.

'My patience run out,' he complained to my mother. 'I is not Job, nuh.'

From the Chinese shop he came back with a green bottle shaped like a banana.

'Aha, this is the fuss and last time for that thief,' he swore. 'They gone too far this time.'

'What you going to do with that baby bottle, Mr Clayton?'

'Boy, I paying you a whole big penny not to bother big people with you chupid question. When school open, ask you teacher questions. Next time you ask chupid questions, I go give you two hot slap, one slap on each side of you face, and it go burn you more than them hot peppers.'

I held my breath. Did he suspect me?

'I paying you a whole big penny for what?' he thundered. 'Cause in this two last weeks, you let them bad boys steal mey cashew nuts, mey dried coconuts, mey mangoes, mey oranges and even mey peppers behind the pig pen. But, now they touch the forbidden fruit. They think I born yesterday? Or I blind like Mr Lomas? But this bottle going to capture the real thief.'

Mr Clayton held up the green bottle to the sunlight.

I studied the bottle which tapered in a narrow neck at each end. I knew mothers put two nipples one on each end and fed their babies from one of the nipples they pricked with a long heated needle.

The next day Mr Clayton was busy pasting the green bottle with some yellow polish, the kind he pasted on his canvas shoes.

'From now on this bottle going to be my new watchman.'

Though I felt he had gone crazy with his old wives' tale, I yet begged Mr Clayton not to fire me. All I was thinking about was the green fountain pen the Chinese shopkeeper promised to knock a whole penny off.

But Mr Clayton said nothing to me as he rode away to sell his fruits.

What could that yellow bottle do? My teacher from the city often laughed about this piece of village black magic.

The bottle glittered in the sunshine almost blinding me. It hung by a yellow cord from the stem of the bunch and looked like a banana itself. Perhaps my neighbour believed some boy would take the bottle for a banana, bite into it, and break all his teeth.

Very funny, I smiled as I vaulted over the fence, and twisted off yet another banana from the back of the bunch. Then, tapping the bottle, I saw water moving to and fro like waves in the sea. 'Maybe Mr Clayton thinks a baby is stealing his bananas.' I laughed and greedily bit off a large chunk of the banana not quite ripe yet.

Footsteps, and quickly I swallowed in large lumps the whole banana, and hid the greenish peel under my bed.

Earlier than usual my mother had come home from the sugarcane fields where from between rows of sugarcane beds she plucked weeds or sprinkled salts at the roots of the young sugarcane for fifty cents a week.

Just then, too, Mr Clayton came rolling in his bicycle, which he leaned against a coconut tree, and tramped through the bushes directly to the banana tree. He loosened the cord, and swung the bottle to and fro. 'The sea is rough – the waves are high!' he shouted jubilantly. 'Soon the village shall know the thief!'

My mother stopped her sweeping and rushed to the window.

Up and down the road Mr Clayton was howling, showing off the bottle. 'Another worst day for Waterloo,' he cried aloud. 'Tha thiefing boy had better come forward. He stole my bananas. And the sea-in-the-bottle was on the banana tree.'

My mother was looking at me as I stood outside our gate looking at the village children flocking around Mr Clayton swinging the bottle before his eyes.

'See this bottle. I filled it with sea water. Yes, this bottle is filled with salt water from the sea. Now you all knows that the tide rise in the early morning and again the tide rise in the late evening.'

I held back laughing aloud. But my stomach began aching, and I doubled over.

'Speak up!' Mr Clayton bellowed. 'Which one of you children stole mey banana? Speak before it is too late. For before the sun goes down today, I will ride down to the sea and toss this bottle deep down into the water. When the tide rise, the belly of the thief will also rise.'

Down in my stomach I felt more stabbing pains.

'When the tide go out and fall, the belly of the thief will flatten out normal again,' he harangued.

Fearfully boys and girls looked to one another. Wildly they begged the other to confess. Some of the girls began crying while the boys began looking suspiciously one to the other.

'Up and down for the rest of his life the belly of banana thief will rise and fall like the tide!'

I gulped down air, my stomach churning like an angry sea.

'Dear children of Waterloo, confess your sin. Please, I am begging you. For when I tosses this bottle into the sea what happen to Widow Crichtlow onliest son will happen to one of you. You thief mey plums, mey papaya, mey cashew nuts, even mey green peppers. But there was no curse on them trees.'

My mother shouted: 'Come right dis minute in dis house, Sunshine. Stop listening to what doesn't concern you. Let the guilty person pay for they own sin. I has to sweep under you bed.'

Too late for me.

The next moment my mother with the banana peel in her hand was chasing after Mr Clayton just as he was about to ride off with the bottle down to the sea.

'Please, neighbour Clayton, spare my boy. I'm a poor widow. Who will see about me in my old age? Please, don't throw that bottle into the sea, and curse Sunshine for the rest of he life.'

Mr Clayton hopped off his bicycle.

My mother, dragging me by the hair, while I held on to my stomach, began whacking me with the broom.

'I promise you, neighbour that this untruthful boy go water you garden twice daily, till school open again, if you will only spare this wotliss boy.'

Mr Clayton scratched his head, narrowing his eyes at me.

'This wotliss boy make a fool out of a big man for too long,' Mr Clayton said, rolling the bottle about in his palms. 'Then Sunshine gone and make me falsely blame these innocents children here.'

He turned to the boys and girls: 'Can you trust a friend who tells untruth, who tell sinful lies to you?'

Not one of them answered but stonily fixed their eyes upon me so that I felt like crawling into the bottle.

My mother dealt me another loud blow.

A lump of banana popped up out of my mouth.

In a chorus, singing 'Banana boy!' all the boys and girls mocked and teased, running off, in two's and three's, and continued chanting through the village that Sunshine was the banana thief.

My mother was crying. 'I give you my blessed word, neighbour Clayton. If this little lying boy just miss one day watering you fruit trees, I myself go throw him and – and that bottle in the sea.'

My neighbour seemed very pleased.

Later that afternoon my mother twisting my ears, dragged me across to the pink hut of Mr Clayton.

'To show you, neighbour, that this boy mean to keep his promise, Sunshine has come to give you back all the pennies he didn't honestly work for.'

The Brothers and the Witch

Ian Fellowes Gordon

*So many of the well-confirmed tales of the supernatural have as their settin
either the extreme north or the extreme south of the British Isles that one
inclined towards the theory that occult and supernatural beings prefer the wilde
coastal settings. Be that as it may, the following events have been told so ofte
and are so firmly established in local lore that many Cornishmen believe i
their reality as firmly as they do in the historical reality of, say, the Duke o
Wellington — who, it just happens, was achieving high fame at the time.*

IT WAS AN AUTUMN EVENING IN THE YEAR 1810; AND THE TOW
was Helston, where the Lizard peninsula can be said to begin
The peninsula leads down to the Lizard Point, the most southerl
feature of England's mainland. Helston is the home of the famou
Flora dance and was later in the century to claim as one of it
sons, the boxer, Bob Fitzsimmons.

Two apprentice saddlers, Charlie and Jim Williams, were in their attic bedroom in one of the roads off the steep high street, rather uncomfortably perched on stools.

'But what's wrong, Charlie?'

'Nothing. It's nothing at all. Just that I'm not tired. I don't see why, just because we're apprentices, we have to be in bed by nine. I could stay up for hours. We could have a game of cards, now, couldn't we?'

Jim, the elder brother, all of thirteen years, but a strapping lad, almost a man, looked at his eleven-year-old younger brother. Why, if ever a boy needed eight hours between the blankets, it was little Charlie Williams. There were great black shadows under each eye, the complexion was pale, almost grey.

'Never mind, Charlie. I think Mr and Mrs Carver know what's best for us. And in a year or two, we'll be our own masters, able to get to bed when we want.'

'I suppose so. But I still don't want to go to bed. Not here – in the Carvers' house. I have terrible dreams, Jim.'

'That's because you eat too much things last night. A huge great slab of Mrs Carver's bread and cheese isn't the thing to dream on. And washed down with her ale. You're too young for that. Just try cutting down on the grub.'

'Oh! all right.' Young Charlie threw the last bit of bread and cheese into the fireplace.

It had taken the boys a month or so to get used to the Carvers. Helston was quite a distance from their home at Marazion and Mr Carver had at first seemed gruff, almost hostile, and definitely so when the boys made stupid mistakes. 'Saddler can't suffer fools gladly, lad. It's more than the business is worth, having shoddy work turned out.'

But a moment later Mr Carver was all smiles. 'I'm sorry, lads. I get a bit gruff sometimes. But I like the pair of you. Sure you're getting enough to eat?'

'Oh yes, sir. And thank you, Mrs Carver, it was a beautiful supper, really it was.'

The cosy Mrs Carver, roughly as wide as she was high, would then embrace the boys in turn.

So it was a happy enough life. But this new hatred of going to bed which was being shown by young Charlie Williams worried his elder brother. He would lie in the next bed, unable to sleep while the younger brother seemed to fight the onslaught of sleep. Usually Jim was asleep before the muttering and the rolling in the next bed had stopped.

The next morning he was, for the first time, horrified at his younger brother's appearance. The boy was ashen and his lips were trembling so that he could hardly speak.

'Now Charlie, you must tell me. What are these dreams you're having?'

'It's nothing. Tonight – well, I won't have any supper at all, not a morsel. And if I have the same dream, I'll tell you about it'

'The same dream? Why, do you always have the same one?'

'Yes.'

'But you've got to tell me now. The dreams are exactly the same?'

'Not exactly. But almost. And they're – they're awful—'

To the older boy's dismay, young Charlie burst into tears and cried as if his heart would break. Jim held him tight, and eventually the weeping stopped. 'I'm sorry. Just being a cry-baby.'

'No, you're not. We all get to cry a little, now and then. But you mark my words, if you're like this tomorrow morning,

I'm getting Mr Carver to fetch the doctor. He'll give you some physic, and that'll put you right.'

'Very well. Tell you about it tomorrow, if it happens again.'

The day passed fairly uneventfully, except that the dog-tired Charlie made more mistakes than usual and Mr Carver was obviously holding himself in rein. Jim took him aside. 'It'll be all right, Mr Carver, sir. Charlie just hasn't been sleeping. And if it's the same tonight, I'll ask you if you'd be getting the physician to see him.'

'Physician? But don't you think, Jim my lad, that it's maybe just homesickness? I could always send him home to your parents for a few days, there's a stagecoach or diligence leaves quite often—'

'I don't think it's homesickness, Mr Carver.'

Mr Carver was concerned. Perhaps the boy was not getting enough to eat and drink, and that would be a terrible disgrace. Mrs Carver would make sure he got a really good supper from now on. And though he didn't approve of young lads having much ale at the best of times, maybe a mug or two more of it might give the lad a good night's sleep. Certainly did for him: an extra quart and he slept as if he'd been hit with a blacksmith's hammer. That is, until he had to get up and run some of it off, of course.

He intimated these thoughts to Jim.

'We'll see, sir. I think maybe tonight he ought to have a very light supper, just as a try-out, you might say. And then I'll tell you about it in the morning.'

That night the two brothers went to bed at the usual hour, both of them rather hungry. For at least half an hour Jim Williams stayed awake, hoping to hear the peaceful breathing of a younger brother being welcomed into the arms of Morpheus. But he was tired from his own exertions in the saddler's workshop and he fell asleep, leaving Charlie still tossing and turning.

In the morning he was again shocked at his brother's appearance. Without wasting time, even before they got out of their little wooden beds, he demanded the full story. 'Come on. I'm going to hear all about this dream, every bit.'

'You wouldn't believe it.'

'That's for me to judge.'

'All right, then. Well, it happens just the same way every night. Don't even know whether I'm awake or asleep when it happens—'

'When what happens?'

'You see this bed of mine's nearer the door than yours is. Every night a horrible woman comes in that door, makes straight for my bed—'

'What's she look like? Like Mrs Carver?' To Jim's delight, he managed to draw a pale smile over the other's features.

'No, but she is fat. She seems to be dressed in brown or black, though it's hard to see, really. And her long, sort of grey-black, hair, it's piled on her head like a bun. Reminds me of someone round these parts, but, well, I just can't remember exactly. But she's terribly strong, grabs me by the neck. I can't possibly call out or do anything. And yet she weighs – she hardly weighs anything at all. She gets to fix a bridle, right over my head. I think it must be one of Mr Carver's—'

'Slips a bridle over your head?'

'Yes. And a bit between my teeth. Jim, she's so strong I can't possibly stop her; and she gets on my back and kicks me on either side, just like you kick a horse. Then she makes me carry her round the end of your bed and out through the window; and though we're way up in the air, she seems to get me flying, turns me into a sort of flying horse. And out we go, her riding on my back—'

Under Jim's insistent questioning the rest of the story came out. They rode great distances, but Charlie could not say exactly where. He had a vague idea it was north of the Helford River in the direction of St. Mawes.

After about an hour's galloping flight they arrived at the witch's destination – her coven – for there were other witches there. It was a very bleak foreshore between two giant rocks. Here she tied him up to a rotting post, and then started to babble with the other witches. Something foul was always being cooked.

'You never get any of it?'

'Oh no! I should be sick.'

'And then what happens?'

'Then she unties me from the post, gets on my back, kicks me in the ribs and we head back here to Helston again. We sail down the high street, and straight in through the window. She gets off and very quietly leads me past the end of your bed, drags me into my own and takes off my bridle. And then—'

'Yes?'

'Then she kisses me. I think this is the worst part of all. She kisses me and she goes out – through the closed door. Oh, Jim, it's horrible, it really is.'

And indeed it must be. Jim knew the ring of truth in his brother's voice and he could feel his own heart beat fast at the horror of it.

There was only one thing to do. 'Charlie,' he announced quietly, 'we shall change beds tonight.'

Charlie demurred, for he was fond of his elder brother, and hated the idea of his having the same ghastly experience. However the rejoinder was firm.

'Remember I'm two years older than you and everyone says I'm big and strong for my age. So I'd like to have a tussle with this witch of yours.'

'But don't you think, now we both know about it, we ought to tell Mr and Mrs Carver?'

'Maybe. But not until after tonight.'

That day the brothers worked especially hard and Mr Carver noted that although the younger one was still pale and sickly looking, they both whistled from time to time as they worked. And their work was fine and accurate too. He felt constrained to congratulate them. 'You're doing a fine job, lads. I think you'll make good saddlers, the pair of you.'

The boys mumbled their thanks and went on with the work of stitching two bridles. Jim found himself looking at all the bridles on the wall and wondering if any of these had been used by the witch. But no, they were all brand-new, beautiful bridles, and they could never have been taken down from their hooks.

That evening, sharp at the usual time, they went up to their room. Charlie had been prevailed upon to have a large supper, thick soup with a large pasty, and also almost a quart of beer. Jim, unsmiling, partook of hardly anything, and the Carvers watched with interest as the two of them went up the narrow winding stairs from the kitchen.

'They're a rum pair, those two,' said Mr Carver.

'Oh, they're just boys,' said his wife. 'We mustn't worry about them. Did you see how much the little one tucked away tonight? I was proper delighted.'

'And the big one had hardly anything. Strange —'

As arranged, the boys swopped beds, Charlie Williams tonight climbing into the one furthest from the door. And to his older brother's satisfaction he was soon fast asleep.

He was unaware what time he himself dropped off, and never was really clear later on just how long he had slept.

But he suddenly awoke with a feeling of great oppression upon him. He looked up and saw the old woman, bending over his bed – and there really was a bridle in her hand. Her grey face was lit by the moon streaming in through the bedroom window, and he could see that she was indeed rather fat, had her hair piled up in a ramshackle bun and was more or less entirely covered by a hideous, shapeless, black or brown dress of a coarse material, with a little black cloak about her shoulders. Her round face was not really malevolent, and she did, as Charlie had hinted, remind one of somebody, somebody one had seen, maybe in Helston.

He let the bridle be slipped over his head and he even took the bit between his teeth. Obedient to the rider's signals, he lifted her towards the window, feeling her calloused heels dig deep into his ribs. Charlie had been right, and despite her shape and strength, she was weightless.

Jim already had his plan. He would wait, though, until they had flitted out through the attic window: there'd be no point in waking up poor Charlie. Let him get a decent night's sleep tonight, and Jim would make sure he got one every night from now on.

Out of the window they floated. It was rather like swimming through the night air, and Jim found that his limbs took up the motion naturally as if he'd been carrying weightless witches all his life. In a way, until the fat old thing gave a vicious tweak to the reins, which hurt his mouth, it was quite pleasant, just swimming through that moon-bright autumn air with something weightless on his back. Weightless – and so fat!

Then, when they were well away from the house, he did it.

There was a terrible scream from the old hag as he dragged her down off his back with one hand and took the bit from between his teeth with the other. But she was so light, even though she had strength, that he had no difficulty in getting her off his back, changing places with her. The bit fitted well in her jaws.

'Get moving,' he shouted in triumph. 'Tonight it's my turn to ride, and I want to go fast. We've got a long journey. First to Porthleven, then off to Mullion Cove. After that down the coast past Kynance to the Lizard Point. And we'll come back up the other side over Cadgwith and St Keverne. Across the Goonhillie Downs – they should be fine and misty and wonderful tonight – back here to Helston. And if you don't go fast enough, I'll just kick you till you do.'

He did, and there was a grunt of pain.

'Come on, now. I want to be back in my bed by dawn.'

He could see where they were and after describing an aerial arc around Porthleven, to his surprise the old woman descended the few feet to ground level, was actually galloping, like a horse, down the Lizard road.

And as they galloped on, she slowly began to take on the shape of a real horse. First her strange hair divided on the top of her head and became horse's ears. And the short cloak in front of him changed slowly into a long black mane. If he looked down he could see the short fat fingers, the shapeless shoes, becoming pairs of horse's hooves.

Surely no racehorse in history had travelled so far. The sound of its hooves was like the rattle of a drum-roll, and it grew faster.

They were already in mist, the strange fascinating sea mist of the Predannack downs, where a rider's head can be above it and the rest of him and his horse quite hidden. Occasionally the top of a tree, one of the very few trees in that barren land, or the roof of a house, appeared above it and shot by. At Ruan Minor they turned off to Mullion, had a fine view from the cove of the grey, slow-breaking sea across to Mounts Bay; then stormed on past Kynance to the Lizard itself. The moon gave an eerie polish to everything and he had the strange feeling of riding on the blanket of mist.

He was singing with the exhilaration of the night air and the speed, when he suddenly noticed his steed was limping.

The galloping eased to a limping canter, then a walk. Jim dismounted carefully, holding tight to the reins, to inspect.

It was as he had thought. The shoes were worn almost through and one of them was hanging by only a pair of nails. He owed the witch no kindness, God knew, but common sense told him he must wake up some blacksmith and get a new set of shoes put on. Already there was a pale glow in the east, and if he didn't make haste, he and his horse-witch would not be back by dawn.

As luck would have it, he found an early-risen smith working at his bellows in St. Keverne. He stopped his steed and watched as the puffing and huffing blew life into the embers by the anvil. Then he dismounted, still holding the animal firmly by its reins.

'Excuse me,' he said nervously, suddenly feeling a thirteen-year-old boy again, not a champion rider, a tamer of witches.

'Yes?' said the smith.

'Could you – would you – shoe my horse for me? We've come a long way and she's lame.'

Jim had not had occasion to ascertain the sex of his steed, but presumably it would be a mare.

'Aye, I'll do that for you,' said the smith.

'Thank you very much. It's very kind of you, at this hour of the morning.'

'Oh, that's all right. Money's money, whether the sun shines or the moon. You have got money, have you? To me, you look as if you'd just scrambled out of bed in your nightdress.'

Jim had a moment of panic, then remembered. 'This is the way I like to ride at night, in these clothes. More freedom. They're not really nightclothes, of course. And I have money, in this leathern bag around my neck.'

He took out some silver coins from the bag he always wore this way day and night, and they glistened in the red light from the glowing coals.

The smith got to work. 'My, these shoes have worn a fair way. You'd not get much further with the likes of these. I've never seen such shoes, not even slippers, they aren't—' The man laughed at his little joke and Jim nervously laughed with him.

The four new shoes were fitted, the nails hammered home, and Jim paid the obliging smith, who took rather less than the youth had imagined the job was worth. 'Good luck,' he said. 'Good luck, young fellow. And get safely home – before your folks see what you've been doing. I must say, though, I admire a lad with spirit—'

Jim mounted his horse-witch and galloped away, as the genial smith waved farewell. The beast was running beautifully now, which was just as well, for the sky was becoming quite light.

They reached the Carvers' house in the side street.

'Right,' said Jim. 'I want you to change back into a witch – or I'll kick you real hard – and jump back into that attic window. And not a sound, understand?'

Obediently, the ears became hair again – a bun – and the rest of the horse became the rest of an old woman. One bound and they were through the window, Jim clinging on for dear life.

'And now get out,' hissed Jim at the woman, 'Get out, and never come back.' The woman paused for a moment, then turned and slowly went out through the closed door.

Charlie woke, stretched himself. Jim had already slithered into the next bed.

'Oh Jim, I had a wonderful night's sleep. Not a nightmare, not even a dream, nothing. It was fine.'

'Good. I had a pleasant night, too.' Jim had decided not to tell the younger boy what had happened, lest it upset him and he started having dreams of a different nature. 'No, I didn't dream either. But I think we'll stay in these beds from now on.'

Helston was beginning to stir to a new day, and they could hear the Carvers busying themselves below, making breakfast, starting work. And then, in the distance, came a scream.

It grew louder and louder and they heard Mr Carver put down something heavy in his workshop and go out at the double, up Helston's precipitous high street. The screaming went on.

By the time he got back to the house the boys were up and dressed, and it was their master's turn to look haggard and distraught.

'What is it? What is it, John Carver?' asked his wife. 'You look as if you'd seen a ghost—'

'My God, perhaps worse. There's been a fat old woman hanging around at the top of the high street for some weeks now. Nobody seemed to know where she came from, even where she stays. Quite a friendly body, they say, but, well, there's something a bit uncanny, unpleasant about her.'

'Oh, come to the point, John Carver.'

'Well, believe me or believe me not, this old hag's sitting there on the ground, screaming her head off in agony. And small wonder. There's a brand-new horse-shoe nailed tight on to each hand and foot.'

The Outlaws' Report

Richmal Crompton

The first 'William' stories appeared in 1921, and he continued to entertain children and adults well over thirty years. In this 1945 story he draws up a petition demanding shorter school hours – among other things . . .

WILLIAM PLODDED ALONG THE ROAD, HIS SCHOOL SATCHEL OVER his shoulder, his hands in his pockets. He was collecting keys for metal salvage, and so far he had met with fairly good results. Large keys, little keys, rusty keys, bright keys, door keys, cupboard keys, attaché-case keys, jewel-case keys, ignition keys, jingled behind him as he walked. . . . But he wasn't thinking of keys. He was thinking of the conversations he had overheard at the houses where he had visited. They had nearly all been on the same topic. . . . 'Reconstruction' . . . 'better conditions' . . . 'shorter hours' . . . 'higher wages' . . . 'freedom from want and fear' . . .

'the Beveridge Report'. . . . His brow was deeply furrowed as he plodded along to the old barn, where he had arranged to meet the other Outlaws and compare results in key collecting.

Ginger, Douglas and Henry were already there when he arrived, engaged in counting their spoils.

'We've got over a hundred altogether so far,' said Ginger excitedly. 'How many have you got, William?'

William dumped his satchel down in a corner, still frowning abstractedly.

'Dunno,' he said. 'Look here! Everyone's talkin' about better conditions an' shorter hours an' things, an' what I want to know is what's goin' to happen to us?'

'What about?' said Henry.

'Well, everyone else is goin' to get a jolly good time after the war, but no one's thinkin' of us. Jus' 'cause we've not got a vote or anythin' we're not goin' to come in for any of it. What about shorter hours an' more money an' all the rest of it for us? I bet we could do with a bit of freedom from want an' fear, same as anyone else.'

'Yes, I bet we could,' agreed the others.

'I don't see why grown-ups should get everything an' us nothin'.

'How do grown-ups get it?' asked Douglas.

'They've got a thing called a Beveridge Report,' explained William.

'Why can't we have one?'

'This Beveridge man's grown-up,' said William bitterly. 'So he only cares about grown-ups. We've gotter do somethin' for ourselves if we want anythin' done at all.'

'The Outlaws' Report,' suggested Henry.

'Yes, that's it. The Outlaws' Report. . . . An' we'd better get it goin' pretty quick. . . . Let's go to your house, Ginger. It's the nearest.'

In Ginger's bedroom they squatted down on the floor to compose the terms of the Outlaws' Report, and Ginger tore the two middle pages from his Latin exercise-book and handed them to William.

'That'll do to write it down on,' he said. 'We've gotter have it same as theirs. . . .'

'Well, first of all, they're goin' to have shorter hours,' said William. 'So we'll have 'em too.'

'Longer holidays,' said Ginger.

'Much longer holidays,' said Henry.

'As much holidays as term,' said Douglas.

'More holidays than term,' said Ginger.

'We'd better not ask for too much,' said William, 'or we may not get it. We'll ask for as much holidays as term. That's only fair. Well, it stands to reason that, when we've wore out our brains, for say, three months, we oughter have three months for our brains to grow back to their right size again. Well, you've only gotter think of trees an things vaguely. They've got all winter to rest in. Their leaves come off at the end of summer an' don't come on again till the nex' summer, an' I bet our brains oughter be as important as a lot of ole leaves.'

The Outlaws, deeply impressed by the logic of this argument, assented vociferously.

'Holidays as long as term,' wrote William slowly and laboriously.

'An' no afternoon school,' suggested Ginger.

'Yes, no afternoon school,' agreed William. 'Afternoon school's not nat'ral. Well, come to that, school's not nat'ral at all. Look at animals. They don't go to school an' they get on all right. Still, I don't s'ppose they'd let us give up school altogether, 'cause of school masters havin' to have somethin' to do. Axshally, I don't see why schoolmasters shouldn't teach each other. It'd give 'em somethin' to do an' serve 'em right. Still, we'll be reas'nable. We'll jus' put down holidays as long as term an' no afternoon school.' . . . Then there's "Higher Wages."'

'Yes,' said Ginger, 'that's jolly important. I could do with a bit of higher wages, all right.'

'Let's say, sixpence a week pocket money,' suggested Henry.

'An' not to be took off for anythin',' said Ginger. 'They're always takin' mine off me for nothin' at all. Jus' meanness. I bet they've made pounds out of me, takin' my pocket money off for nothin' at all.'

'Yes, we'll put that in,' said William, and wrote: 'Sixpence a week pocket munny, and not to be took off.' 'Now, what comes next? What other better conditions do we want?'

'No Latin,' said Ginger firmly.

'No French,' said Douglas.

'No Arithmetic,' said Henry.

'No, none of them,' agreed William firmly, adding this fresh demand to the list. 'I bet we can get on without them, all right.'

'What about no hist'ry?' suggested Ginger.

'Well, we've gotter keep somethin' for school masters to teach,' said William indulgently. 'Hist'ry isn't bad, an' English isn't bad, 'cause ole Sarky can't see what you're doin' at the back, an' Stinks isn't bad, 'cause you can get some jolly good bangs if you mix the wrong things together. We'll jus' keep it at, "No Latin or French or Arithmetic."'

'What else is there?' said Henry.

'Well, they're very particular about "Freedom from Want an' Fear,"' said William. 'We've gotter be particular about that, too.'

'That means no punishments,' said Douglas.

'Yes, that's only fair,' said William. 'They can break things an' be late for meals an' get cross and forget things an' answer each other back an' do what they like an' nothin' ever happens to them, so I don't see why it should to us. It's about time we had a bit of this equality what people are always talkin' about.'

'Well, let's put that down,' said Ginger. 'No punishments and stay up as late as we like.'

'An' what about food?' said Douglas. 'We'd better put down somethin' about that. We need somethin' more than sixpence a week to give us freedom from want. I bet I wouldn't feel free from want – not really, not honestly free from want – without six ice creams a day.'

'An' bananas – after the war.'

'An' cream buns.'

'Yes, an' cream buns.'

'An' bulls' eyes. Lots an' lots of them. As many as we want.'

'An' we can't buy all that out of sixpence a week, so it ought to be extra.'

'Yes, it jolly well oughter be extra.'

They contemplated this blissful prospect in silence for some moments, then William said, 'Now let's get it all put down prop'ly. Give us another piece of paper, Ginger.'

Ginger tore several more sheets from the middle of his mutilated Latin exercise-book.

'It won't matter,' he said carelessly, "cause we won't be doin' Latin any more after we get this Report thing fixed up.'

William took a sheet and wrote: 'Outlaws' Report' at the head of it.

'They're goin' to make this Beveridge Report thing into an Act of Parliament,' he said, 'so we oughter do somethin' about gettin' ours made into one.'

'What can we put that means that?' asked Ginger.

They all looked at Henry, who was generally considered the best informed of the Outlaws.

'I think it's Habeas Corpus,' said Henry. 'That's somethin' to do with it anyway.'

'No, it isn't. It's Magna Charta,' said Douglas. 'I'm sure it's Magna Charta.'

'We'll put both in,' said William pacifically, 'so as to be on the safe side. How do you spell 'em?'

'Dunno,' said Douglas and Henry, who never liked to own himself at a loss, said airily. 'Oh, jus' as they're pronounced.'

Carefully, laboriously, William wrote:

Outlaws Report.

    Habby. Ass. Corpuss.

    Magner Carter.

    1. As much holidays as term.

    2. No afternoon school.

    3. Sixpence a week pocket munny and not to be took off.

    4. No Latin, no French, no Arithmetic.

5. As much ice-cream and bananas and cream buns as we like free.
6. No punishments and stay up as late as we like.

He looked up from his labours, frowning intently.

'Is there anythin' else?' he said.

The Outlaws drew deep breaths of ecstasy.

'No,' said Ginger in a trance-like voice, 'if we get that, it'll be all right. We'll be freed from want an' fear then, all right.'

'Well, what do we do about it now?' said William.

They awoke slowly and reluctantly from dreams of unlimited ice-cream, bananas and holidays. . . .

'We've gotter get it made into an Act of Parliament,' said Ginger. 'How do we start?'

'Well,' said Henry rather uncertainly, 'I suppose we've got to write to the Government about it.'

'That wouldn't be any good,' said William. 'It never is. D'you remember when we wrote to the Government asking them to let us be commandos, an' they never even answered? An' the time we wrote to them askin' them to shut all the schools an' send all the school masters out to the war to finish it off quick, 'cause of them all bein' so savage, an' they never even answered that.'

'We ought to take it to Parliament ourselves.'

'They wouldn't let us in.'

'Then we ought to give it to a Member of Parliament to take.'

'That wouldn't be any good. There's only one Member of Parliament round here, and he's been mad at us ever since we tried to turn his collie into a French poodle.'

'Then we've gotter find someone else high-up who's goin' to London to see the Government and will take it for us.'

'I know!' said Ginger with a sudden shout. 'There's Major Hamilton. He's high-up in the War Office, an' he's been home for the week end, an' he's going back this mornin'. Let's ask him to take it.'

The Outlaws' faces glowed with eagerness, then gradually the glow faded.

'That wouldn't be any good,' said Douglas with a pessimism born of experience. 'People don't take any notice of children. It's jus' 'cause this ole Beveridge man's grown-up, that they make all this fuss of him. Ours is jus' as good, but I bet they won't take any notice of it.'

'Let's go an' see, anyway,' said William. 'Where does he live?'

'Up at Marleigh,' said Ginger. 'He might be sens'ble enough to see that it's jus' as necess'ry for children to have improved conditions as what it is for grown-ups, but, of course,' he ended gloomily, 'he might not.'

William folded up the document, slipped it into an envelope, wrote, 'Outlaws Report. Pleese give to Parlyment' on the outside, and put it carefully into his pocket, then, accompanied by the other three Outlaws, made his way across the fields to Marleigh.

There, in front of a square Georgian house, stood a car laden with luggage.

'That's it,' said Ginger excitedly. 'That's where he lives an' he's goin' back to London today. His mother told mine he was.'

A man with red tabs on the shoulders of his uniform hurried down to the car, threw a bag on to the top of the other bags and returned to the house.

He wore a lofty, supercilious expression, with a short moustache and an eyeglass.

'He looks high-up, all right,' said William.

'But he doesn't look as if he'd take much notice of us,' said Ginger, his excitement giving place to despondency.

'No, he doesn't,' said William, inspecting him. 'He doesn't look as if he'd even let us explain.'

'He's got some jolly important papers with him,' said Ginger. 'He brought 'em home to go over, an' he's takin' them back with him today. His mother tellin' mine that.'

'Gosh!' said William excitedly. 'Tell you what we could do! We could jus' slip our Report in with his papers an' it would go to the Government with them an' be made an Act of Parliament. That's a jolly good idea.'

'But how're we goin' to slip it in with them?'

William surveyed the back of the car, piled up with cases and rugs.

'I bet they're somewhere there,' he said. 'I bet I could find them if I had a good look. I'll get in an' have a try, anyway.'

With that, William crept up to the car, opened the door, and, crouching under a large rug that was hanging down untidily from the back seat, began his investigations among the cases that were piled there. Almost immediately Major Hamilton came down the garden path, leapt into the driving seat, waved his hand carelessly towards the house and started the car. It drove off, leaving the three remaining Outlaws staring after it, their faces petrified by horror.

William was only slightly perturbed. The car would be sure to stop somewhere for petrol or something, and then, having slipped his Report in among Major Hamilton's other important papers, he would make his way back as best he could. In fact, the element of adventure in the situation was rather exhilarating than otherwise. . . . Very quietly – so as not to attract the attention of the driver – he continued to burrow among the cases. A locked attaché-case seemed the most likely receptacle. Remembering the satchel of keys that he still carried over his shoulder, he took it off and searched among it. Several keys seemed to be of suitable size. He tried them, one after another. The last one fitted. He opened the case. Yes, it was full of papers that looked important. He decided to put the Outlaws' Report at the bottom, so that it should be taken out with the others, and not attract attention till it was presented to the Government along with them and, with luck, made automatically into an Act of Parliament. Turning the other papers out carelessly, he bundled them into his satchel, with a faint realisation of the fact that, though less important than the Report, they were still important, and must be kept carefully till they could be replaced in the attaché-case. He tried the Report in every position and at every angle, in order to find out which looked most impressive – right way up, with the words 'Outlaws Report. Pleese Give to Parlyment' boldly displayed . . . wrong way up . . . sideways . . . corner ways. . . .

Suddenly the car began to slow down. Concerned for the safety of his precious manuscript, William hastily locked the attaché-case, then, concerned for his own safety, crouched beneath the rug. . . .

The car stopped, and William, peeping from a corner of the rug, saw that it had drawn up in front of a hotel. Major Hamilton got out of the car and entered the hotel. William considered his next step. He had done what he had come to do, so he might as well return home before he was discovered. The Report was now on its way to the Government in London . . . and presumably something would be done about it sooner or later.

Very cautiously, he slipped out of the car (on the side away from the hotel) and set off down the road. He'd probably find out where he was from a post office or something. He might even be able to 'hitch hike' home, which would be a novel and enjoyable experience. A motor cyclist passed him, going at a breakneck speed. William put out his hand to stop him, but received only a scowl in reply. Oh well, probably something else would pass him soon, and he'd try again.

He walked on for a short distance then stopped, stunned by a sudden recollection. He'd still got Major Hamilton's papers in his satchel. Gosh! He'd better take them back again, or he'd be getting in a row with the Government, and it might even put them against the Outlaws' Report. He mustn't risk that. . . . Hastily he retraced his steps to the car. At the car he found Major Hamilton and a man, who was evidently the manager of the hotel. Major Hamilton looked white and shaken.

'I was only in the hotel a minute or two,' he was saying. 'It was there on the seat of the car – a locked attaché-case – when I went in, and it's gone now. I must get in touch with the police at once.'

'You didn't lock the car?' said the manager.

Major Hamilton grew paler than ever.

'I'd lost the key,' he said. 'I admit I took a chance. As I said, I wasn't in the hotel more than a minute or two and I thought I'd be able to see it from the window. I suppose that someone knew I'd got the papers and had been following me.'

'What's been lost?' said William, pushing himself between them. 'Your attaché-case?'

Major Hamilton looked at him, as if hoping against all reasonable hope that help might be forthcoming even from this unlikely source.

'Yes . . . Do you know anything about it? There were most important papers in it.'

'I should think there were,' said William indignantly. 'There was our Report. Gosh! If that's been stolen. . . .'

'What on earth are you talking about?' said the Major impatiently. 'I'm speaking of important Government papers and. . . .'

'Oh, them!' said William carelessly. 'I've got them all right. I was jus' comin' to put 'em back.'

With that, he slung off his satchel, took out the papers and thrust them into the astonished Major's hand.

'I've got a lot of keys, too,' he continued calmly. 'I bet I could find one to fit your car.'

There were long explanations, at the end of which (a key was actually found to fit the car) the Major took him into the hotel, gave him a meal that seemed to William one of pre-war magnificence and saw him into a bus that would take him home.

'No, I didn't get it to London,' explained William to the Outlaws. 'It was stole before we got there.'

'Gosh!' said the Outlaws, impressed. 'I shouldn't have thought anyone knew enough about it for that.'

'Oh well,' admitted William, 'there were some other papers, too, but I bet it was our Report they were after really. Someone must have found out about it. . . .'

'Then we won't get an Act of Parliament?' said the Outlaws, disappointed.

'Well, p'raps not an Act of Parliament exactly,' admitted William, 'but this Major Hamilton says he'll do the best he can for us. He'll take us to a pantomime at Christmas.'

The Outlaws' drooping spirits soared.

'A pantomime! Gosh!'

'Hurrah!'

For the Outlaws had acquired a certain philosophy of life and realised that a pantomime in the hand is worth a dozen Acts of Parliament in the bush. . . .

From *William and the Brains Trust (1945)*

Auntie

Edward Blishen

*Edward Blishen was a distinguished editor and children's writer, who published
some of my early stories in the anthologies he edited when I was an aspiring
young writer: Here is one of his own memorable stories . . .*

AUNTIE WAS OUR ART MASTER. I THINK HE MUST HAVE BEEN the
oldest Art master in the world. He was immensely thin, and
tall, and such hair as he had – clinging to his otherwise shining
bald head – was as white as fresh May blossom. He also had
moustaches, that drooped on either side of his mouth like big
white commas. When we first met him, Pooh and I had both been
reading a story in which there was a character who turned out
to be two hundred years old. He'd eaten a fungus, or swallowed
some chemical – I can't now remember which it was – and this
had made him immortal. Anyway, after the first lesson we had

with Auntie, Pooh and I turned to one another with the same dreadful question written, as they say, on each of our faces. Could Auntie have eaten a fungus?

I don't exactly know why he was called Auntie. His real name was Mr Searle. Perhaps it was because of his enormous kindliness, so that you have expected that at the end of a lesson he would present you with half a crown, and pat you on the head with his vast bony hand. I'm afraid most of us, most of the time, weren't very kind to him. Art lessons were larks.

Well, to begin with, Auntie's classroom was in an old hut at the end of the playground. The huts had been put up, temporarily, twenty years ago; the school had bought them from the Army. They were wooden, and rather like big drums, so far as noise was concerned; any sound you made was magnified no end of times. We had desks with lids that could be raised and fixed at any angle you wanted with a screw, and of course, if you were careless with the screw the lid would drop with a hollow bang, and the whole hut thundered with the sound. It was the first thing we did, when we went into the hut for an Art lesson: thirty screws were fumbled with, and thirty lids came crashing down. The hut would shake, and a wincing expression would appear on Auntie's kind face. 'Boys!' he would cry. 'Boys, please take more care!' That was Auntie all over; after all his years of teaching, he believed we crashed those desk lids out of sheer clumsiness. So we'd all put on repentant faces, and the lids would go whispering up into position again, and then, somewhere, one would fall back, with a single ringing thud, and everyone would turn to the offender and hiss, 'You idiot! You clumsy idiot! You heard what Auntie said!' And Auntie would beam at us, never seeming to hear that name we improperly applied to him, and he would gesture towards the little arrangement of cubes and cones that was this week's subject for drawing.

It always seemed to be cubes and cones. This baffled us. We thought Art ought to be drawing country scenes, and battles and things of that sort. We weren't with Auntie in his passion for cubes and cones. We didn't share his feeling that getting the shading right, in the matter of cubes and cones, was the essence of Art. We'd all groan, 'Oh, sir, not that again!' And Auntie who must really have been singularly deaf, would smile happily and say, 'You'll see that I've made a new arrangement this week. Slightly more difficult!' Well, we'd think, maybe Auntie could see the difference between one arrangement of cubes and cones and another, but we couldn't. 'It's the same as last week, sir,' we'd shout. And when Auntie went on smiling, one of us would go out and stand close to him and cry, 'It's just the same as last week, sir!' Auntie would look worried and say, 'Oh, I don't think so.' Everyone would stand up, then, and go out to the little table on which the arrangement stood, and push the cubes and cones about, crying, 'That's different, sir!' or, 'Now, that's more like it, Auntie!' And Auntie would flap at us with those huge hands and beg us to sit down and let him work out something that would satisfy us as being really new. Sometimes half a lesson would be taken up with confusion of this kind, the hut booming with our cheerful noise, and, of course, an occasional cube or cone falling to the floor with a big hollow clatter.

When we did at last get to work, groaning and sighing, the next thing that happened was that we broke the tips of our pencils. Auntie was the greatest pencil-sharpener I've ever known. He was really a genius, in that line. A queue would form at his desk of boys holding broken pencils, and Auntie would sit there, very happy, performing very delicately and swiftly with his penknife, and producing on pencil after pencil a point that was absolutely perfect. The thing was to chat with Auntie as you stood there, saying, 'Oh, sir, how do you do it?' And Auntie, who took his perfect pencil-sharpening for granted, would say, 'Eh? What do you mean?' 'How do you get it so beautifully sharp?' we'd say, and Auntie would beam and tell us about the importance of having a sharply pointed pencil. 'You can't get anywhere with a blunt pencil,' he'd say. 'You can't even begin to draw properly with a blunt pencil.' Then we'd ask him about the different kinds of pencil, and what B and HB meant: and though he must have been asked these questions a score of times every week for years, he always answered as though he'd never heard them before. And the boys round the desk would be a sort of screen between Auntie and the rest of the class who were supposed to be drawing, but who in fact would be reading, or talking, or even singing, or swopping their possessions. Yes, Art lessons were larks.

The trouble for Pooh and me was that we liked drawing and were quite good at it. So, though we joined in the fun, we fretted at it, a little; we even took cubes and cones seriously, every now and then. And when Auntie did get round to looking at what we were doing – that is, when the amusement of having your pencil sharpened had died away for a while – he would stand sometimes beside Pooh and me, whose desks were together, and we would talk seriously about Art. That is, we'd talk about shading, and trying to draw so that a cube or a cone on the paper, and didn't just look hat. And one day Pooh said, 'We'd like to draw out in the open, sir – us two. Churches and things like that. Do you think that would be a good thing, sir?'

Well, it was the first I'd heard of it, but Pooh nudged me hard, so, I said nothing, and Auntie smiled and said, 'I think it would be very good for you two to try that. But you'd need an easel.' 'Oh,' said Pooh, 'we could have notebooks and hold them on our knees.' 'An easel would be better,' said Auntie. 'I have an old spare one at home. If you would like to visit my place some evening, I'll give it to you.' 'Oh, could we, sir?' said Pooh. 'That's very kind of you.' And before I could really take in what was happening, he had Auntie's private address written down on a piece of paper, and had agreed that he and I should call there one evening in the following week and collect the easel.

I spoke crossly to Pooh when Auntie had moved on. 'Who said we wanted to draw churches?' I demanded. 'I never said I wanted to draw churches.' Pooh gave me a look I'd grown used to – it was the look he gave me when I said I couldn't come out walking because of homework, or when we were in our local woods and Pooh said we should go into a part that was sealed off with wire and I said obviously we weren't supposed to. Pooh was much bolder than I was. 'Haven't you ever wanted to draw churches, and ponds, and the trees in the woods?' he said. I said all right, but what was it going to be like visiting Auntie's house? What were we doing, visiting a master out of school hours? And Pooh looked very scornful and said it would be fun to see what Auntie was like at home. 'And he's going to give us a real artist's easel,' he said. Then he hit me hard on the arm as he always did to end an argument, and I knew it was no use saying any more.

And that happened to be the lesson when the headmaster came angrily into the hut. He'd been passing, and he'd heard the noise we were making, and he entered in his gown like a sudden bat swooping and then standing there, quivering with rage. Just inside the door a boy called Bonzo -- his real name was Baines -- was down on all fours on the floor, barking; he did this sometimes, I suppose because his nickname had an effect on him now and then, but mostly because it made his friends laugh. Anyway, there he was, on all fours, barking, and the room fell suddenly silent and the barking noise he was making rang out horribly clear and powerful. Bonzo looked up, startled by the silence, and his eye travelled up the headmaster's trouser leg and so up to that angry face. Bonzo scrambled to his feet, trying weakly to look as though being on all fours and barking was a thoroughly proper part of an Art lesson, and the headmaster seized his ear, glared at him, and said: 'You'd better find your seat -- at once, and I think, Master Baines, that you would better let me have five hundred fines by tomorrow morning, without fail. Now sit down, you wretched little boy.' Well, Bonzo slunk red-faced into his seat, and the headmaster glared at us and you could see him sorting out the angry words that filled his mind. Meanwhile, poor Auntie was advancing towards him, a kindly beam of welcome on his face. 'Headmaster,' he said, 'what can I do for you?'

'This won't do, Mr Searle,' said the headmaster. 'This chaos won't do. This noise won't do. These boys are being allowed too much freedom. I am seriously disturbed. I would like to speak to you about it after this lesson, please.' 'Meanwhile' -- and he glared round at us again -- 'who is captain of this wretched form?' Pooh got to his feet, and the headmaster looked him up and down so fiercely that Pooh said afterwards he had the distinct feeling that he'd forgotten to put his head on that morning, or perhaps he'd made an awful mistake in dressing and had put on doublet and hose, or a bathing costume. The headmaster's look was so disapproving, that is. 'You will bring me, young Master Bates,' said the headmaster, 'two hundred lines from each member of this class. I shall expect them on my desk by tomorrow morning.' Then, with a furious nod at Auntie, he stalked out, and for the rest of the lesson we sat in complete silence, trying very hard to get the shading right in the latest arrangement of cubes and cones, and feeling terribly guilty. Because Auntie had gone very white, and now he was sitting at his desk, saying nothing to us, his chin propped in one huge old hand, his eyes fixed on the wall. So bad did we feel that at the end of the lesson Pooh went up to Auntie and said, 'Sorry, sir,' and the old man nodded at him, but not as though he'd really heard what Pooh had said.

Well, it's difficult for boys to go on feeling sorry, like that. By the time the evening came for us to fetch the easel, we'd half forgotten the headmaster's anger and poor Auntie's white face. He lived in a big old house on the edge of the town: it seemed rather a sad place, when we got there. I mean, the garden had obviously been splendid, once, but now it had gone to seed: the paths were weedy, the shrubs were tangled, the trees were untrimmed and made everything dark and damp. We rang the bell and after a time the door opened, and there, in a dark hallway, stood Auntie. He peered at us and then smiled and said, 'Ah, it's you two. Come for the easel. Come in, then. Come in.' We stood there wiping our boots for ages in our nervousness, and then we stepped in – and at once we saw the pictures.

The house was as dark inside as outside, and from the walls great dark pictures were looking down. There were three in the hall, and more as we followed Auntie into a big living-room. At first we couldn't make out what the pictures were about, they were so dim, but then we saw that's what they mostly showed – ▶

mean, dimness. They all seemed to be scenes at night, and mostly
scenes on bridges, in some city or other – you could make out
gloomy buildings in the distance – and there'd usually be a street-
lamp, but not throwing much light, and standing near the lamp
would be a pale-faced girl, or a sad-looking man, or someone in
rags. That's all: just the dark scene and the sad person standing
there, obviously thinking about throwing himself, or herself, in
the river. There was usually a river, under the bridge: I mean,
you could see the sad light of the street-lamp reflected in a ripple
of water. And Pooh, being Pooh, said at once: 'All these pictures,
sir, Did you paint them?' Auntie smiled, very cheerfully, and said,
'Yes. They're all mine.' Then he pointed to the one nearest to
us – pale-faced girl on bridge – and said, 'I submitted that to
the Academy in – oh, a great many years ago, now.' He saw we
looked puzzled and said, 'You know, the Royal Academy. Artists
submit their paintings to be judged and those that the Academy
likes are hung in the annual Exhibition.' 'And did they hang that
one in the Academy?' said Pooh. 'No, no, they didn't hang it,'
said Auntie, quite cheerfully. 'And that one?' said Pooh, pointing
to the next picture. 'I can't remember when I submitted that.
Again quite a long time ago,' said Auntie. Pooh coughed and
said carefully, 'They hung it, sir?' 'No, no,' said Auntie. 'I never
did actually get a picture hung.'

Then he walked across the room, which was terribly untidy,
and tugged at a mass of things leaning against the wall. There
were odd poles, and canvases, and one thing and another; but
what he brought out at last was a fairly huge easel, much bigger
than anything we'd expected, and very heavily made. 'There it
is,' he said, and began to tell us how to use it. Pooh gave me a
quick glance, and I knew him well enough by then to understand

what it meant. 'It's going to be a job to get this home, and to find somewhere to keep it, and I don't know how we're ever going to lug it as far as the woods,' he was thinking, 'but what fun to have an artist's easel as big as this – all our own.'

Well, Auntie had some lemonade ready for us, and as we stood drinking it, Pooh said, very delicately, 'Sir, why did the Academy never take your pictures?' Auntie beamed at us, exactly as though he were telling us about a success instead of a failure, and said, 'I suppose they didn't like them.' 'Oh,' said Pooh, and choked on his lemonade. 'Were they too dark, sir . . . or something?' Auntie looked puzzled. 'Too dark?' he said. Then he looked at us both a little less cheerfully, and said, 'I've always been interested in light and shade. Darkness and light. That's been my interest.' 'Like what you make us do with the . . . cubes and cones, sir?' said Pooh. 'That's the beginning of it,' said Auntie.

Then Pooh said, 'I'm sorry, sir, about the noise we were making the other day – when the headmaster came in.' Whereupon Auntie looked tremendously cheerful again and said, 'Oh, that's all right.' And vaguely he added, 'Boys will be boys.'

We'd finished our lemonade, and we got a grip on that huge easel – one at each end – and Auntie showed us out again into the dark hall, past all the dark, sad pictures the Academy hadn't wanted, and he opened the front door. Suddenly he said, 'I don't think I shall be teaching you much longer. So I hope you'll enjoy using the easel. Remember – light and shade.' Pooh gulped – when we talked it over, we found we were both feeling queerly sad at that moment – and said, 'And keep our pencils sharp, eh, sir?' Auntie frowned, as if he'd been thinking of something else, and then he smiled in his old kind way and said, 'Ah, yes, Bates. Always keep your pencils sharp.'

We were silent for a while as we went jogging through the streets with our immense easel; but after a time we were struck by the comic side of what we were doing – two boys carrying an easel of that size can't have been a common sight in the streets. People turned to stare at us and we began to trot, giggling as we went. By the time we'd got to my house, and had talked to my father and persuaded him to let us keep the easel in the garden shed, we'd almost forgotten the sadness we'd felt in Auntie's house, and the queer feeling all those pictures had given us. . . .

Auntie left us at the end of the term: his place was taken by a very young teacher, who let us use paint galore, and we could draw battles and country scenes to our hearts' content. We saw the cubes and cones only once again – when the new teacher was clearing out Auntie's old cupboard, and came across those dreary objects and called a boy over to him. 'Take this rubbish and drop it in the dustbin, lad,' he said cheerfully. There was never much noise in the hut, after that – the new teacher was very jolly but very firm, and the banging of desk lids was over for ever. The headmaster came in once or twice and looked terribly pleased, and he even praised Bonzo for a painting he was at work on. Everybody said how much better Art was now than it had been with Auntie. But they didn't talk much about that – about the difference, I mean: on the whole, the boys didn't refer to Auntie a great deal. I think they felt a kind of sadness about him, in a vague way. Pooh and I made good use of the easel – it was fine for our drawing expeditions, in the woods and churchyards, and we always enjoyed the fun of trotting it through the streets, with people turning to stare. But, though we never talked about it, there was one thing Pooh and I never failed to do, despite the fact that under the new Art teacher we always used charcoal or drew direct with a brush. We always kept a little store of pencils in our pockets, their points as beautifully sharp as we could make them.

The Children's Crusade

Steven Runciman

This account of a journey from which thousands of children never returned is taken from Sir Steven Runciman's History of the Crusades, published in 1954.

ONE DAY IN MAY 1212, THERE APPEARED AT SAINT-DENIS, WHERE king Philip of France was holding his court, a shepherd-boy of about twelve years old called Stephen, from the small town of Cloyes in the Orleannais. He brought with him a letter for the king, which, he said, had been given to him by Christ in person, who had appeared to him as he was tending his sheep and who had bidden him go and preach the Crusade. King Philip was not impressed by the child and told him to go home. But Stephen, whose enthusiasm had been fired by his mysterious visitor, saw himself now as an inspired leader who would succeed where his elders had failed. For the past fifteen years preachers had been going round the countryside urging a Crusade against the Moslems of the East or of Spain or against the heretics of Languedoc. It was easy for a hysterical boy to be infected with the idea that he too could be a preacher and could emulate Peter the Hermit, whose prowess had during the past century reached a legendary grandeur. Undismayed by the king's indifference, he began to preach at the very entrance to the abbey of Saint-Denis and to announce that he would lead a band of children to the rescue of Christendom. The seas would dry up before them, and they would pass, like Moses through the Red Sea, safe to the Holy Land. He was gifted with an extraordinary eloquence. Older folk were impressed, and children came flocking to his call. After his first success he set out to journey round France summoning the children; and many of his converts went further afield to work on his behalf. They were all to meet together at Vendôme in about a month's time and start out from there to the East.

Towards the end of June the children massed at Vendôme. Awed contemporaries spoke of thirty thousand, not one over twelve years of age. There were certainly several thousand of them, collected from all parts of the country, some of them simple peasants, whose parents in many cases had willingly let them go on their great mission. But there were also boys of noble birth who had slipped away from home to join Stephen and his following of 'minor prophets' as the chroniclers called them. There were also girls among them, a few young priests, and a few older pilgrims, some drawn by piety, others, perhaps, from pity, and others, certainly, to share in the gifts that were showered upon them all. The bands came crowding into the town, each with a leader carrying a copy of the Oriflamme, which Stephen took as the device of the Crusade. The town could not contain them all, and they encamped in the fields outside.

When the blessing of friendly priests had been given, and when the last sorrowing parents had been pushed aside, the expedition started out southward. Nearly all of them went on foot. But Stephen, as befitted the leader, insisted on having a gaily decorated cart for himself, with a canopy to shade him from the sun. At his side rode boys of noble birth, each rich enough to possess a horse. No one resented the inspired prophet travelling in comfort. On the contrary, he was treated as a saint, and locks of his hair and pieces of his garments were collected as precious relics. They took the road past Tours and Lyons, making for Marseilles. It was a painful journey. The summer was unusually hot. They depended on charity for their food, and the drought left little to spare in the country, and water was scarce. Many of the children died by the wayside. Others dropped out and tried to wander home. But at last the little Crusade reached Marseilles.

The citizens of Marseilles greeted the children kindly. Many found houses in which to lodge. Others encamped in the streets. Next morning, the whole expedition rushed down to the harbour to see the sea divide before them. When the miracle did not take place, there was bitter disappointment. Some of the children turned against Stephen, crying that he had betrayed them, and began to retrace their steps. But most of them stayed on by the sea-side, expecting each morning that God would relent. After a few days, two merchants of Marseilles, called, according to tradition, Hugh the Iron and William the Pig, offered to put ships at their disposal and to carry them free of charge, for the glory of God, to Palestine. Stephen eagerly accepted the kindly offer.

Seven vessels were hired by the merchants and the children were taken aboard and set out to sea. Eighteen years passed before there was any further news of them.

Meanwhile, tales of Stephen's preaching had reached the Rhineland. The children of Germany were not to be outdone. A few weeks after Stephen had started on his mission, a boy called Nicholas, from a Rhineland village, began to preach the same message before the shrine of the Three Kings at Cologne. Like Stephen, he declared that children could do better than grown men, and that the sea would open to give them a path. But, while the French children were to conquer the Holy Land by force, the Germans were to achieve their aim by the conversion of the infidel. Nicholas, like Peter, had a natural eloquence, and was able to find eloquent disciples to carry his preaching further, up and down the Rhineland. Within a few weeks an army of children had gathered at Cologne, ready to start out for Italy and the sea. It seems that the Germans were on an average slightly older than the French and that there were more girls with them. There was also a larger contingent of boys of the nobility, and a number of disreputable vagabonds and prostitutes.

The expedition split into two parties. The first, numbering according to the chroniclers, twenty thousand, was led by Nicholas himself. It set out up the Rhine to Basle and through western Switzerland, past Geneva, to cross the Alps by the Mount Cenis pass. It was an arduous journey for the children, and their losses were heavy. Less than a third of the company that left Cologne appeared before the walls of Genoa, at the end of August, and demanded a night's shelter within its walls. The Genoese authorities were at first ready to welcome the pilgrims, but on second thoughts they suspected a German plot. They would allow them to stay for one night only; but any who wished to settle permanently in Genoa were invited to do so. The children, expecting the sea to divide before them the next morning, were content. But next morning, the sea was as impervious to their prayers as it had been to the French at Marseilles. In their disillusion many of the children at once accepted the Genoese offer and became Genoese citizens, forgetting their pilgrimage. Several great families of Genoa later claimed to be descended from this alien immigration. But Nicholas and the greater number moved on. The sea would open for them elsewhere. A few days later they reached Pisa. There two ships bound for Palestine agreed to take several of the children, who embarked and who perhaps reached Palestine; but nothing is known of their fate. Nicholas, however, still awaited a miracle, and trudged on with his faithful followers to Rome. At Rome Pope Innocent received them. He was moved by their piety but embarrassed by their folly. With kindly firmness he told them that they must now go home. When they grew up they should then fulfil their vows and go to fight for the Cross.

Little is known of the return journey. Many of the children, especially the girls, could not face again the ardours of the road, and stayed behind in some Italian town or village. Only a few stragglers found their way back next spring to the Rhineland. Nicholas was probably not amongst them. But the angry parents whose children had perished insisted on the arrest of his father, who had, it seems, encouraged the boy out of vainglory. He was taken and hanged.

The second company of German pilgrims was no more fortunate. It had travelled to Italy through central Switzerland and over the Saint Gotthard and after great hardships reached the sea at Ancona. When the sea failed to divide for them they moved slowly down the east coast as far as Brindisi. There a few of them found ships sailing to Palestine and were given passages; but the others returned and began to wander slowly back again. Only a tiny number returned at last to their homes.

Despite their miseries, they were perhaps luckier than the French. In the year 1230, a priest arrived in France from the East with a curious tale to tell. He had been, he said, one of the young priests who had accompanied Stephen to Marseilles and had embarked with them on the ships provided by the merchants. A few days out they had run into bad weather, and two of the ships were wrecked on the island of San Pietro, off the south-west corner of Sardinia, and all the passengers were drowned. The five ships that survived the storm found themselves soon afterwards surrounded by a Saracen squadron from Africa; and the passengers learned that they had been brought there by arrangement, to be sold into captivity. They were all taken to Bougie, on the Algerian coast. Many of them were bought on their arrival and spent the rest of their lives in captivity there. Others, the young priest among them, were shipped on to Egypt, where Frankish slaves fetched a better price. When they arrived at Alexandria the greater part of the consignment was bought by the governor, to work on his estates. According to the priest, there were still about seven hundred of them living. A small company was taken to the slave markets of Baghdad; and there eighteen of them were martyred for refusing to accept Islam. More fortunate were the young priest and the few others that were literate. The governor of Egypt, al-Adil's son al-Kamil, was terested in Western languages and letters. He bought them and them with him as interpreters, teachers and secretaries, and o attempt to convert them to his faith. They stayed on in

Cairo in a comfortable captivity; and eventually this one priest was released and allowed to return to France. He told the questioning parents of his comrades all that he knew, then disappeared into obscurity. A later story identified the two wicked merchants of Marseilles with two merchants who were hanged a few years afterwards for attempting to kidnap the Emperor Frederick on behalf of the Saracens, thus making them in the end pay the penalty for their crimes.

G. Trueheart, Man's Best Friend

James Mcnamee

Tom Hamilton liked his Aunt Prudence. She taught at the university. Tom's father said she was all brains. Her name was Doctor Prudence Hamilton. When she came to Tom's father's farm in the Cowichan Valley on Vancouver Island, which is part of the Province of British Columbia, she always brought presents. Tom liked her.

He didn't like her constant companion, Genevieve Trueheart, a dog. Tom Hamilton was fond of dogs. He had a dog, a bull terrier called Rusty, a fighter right from the word go. Rusty kept the pheasants out of the garden and the young grain. He worked for a living. Tom couldn't like Genevieve Trueheart. She was good for nothing. She never even looked like a dog. She was a great big soft wheezing lazy wagging monster, a great big useless lump.

Genevieve had been born a Golden Retriever of decent parents and Aunt Prudence had papers to prove it. But Genevieve had eaten so many chocolates and French pastries and frosted cakes that she was three times as wide as a Golden Retriever ought to be. She had the soft muscles of a jellyfish. She couldn't run. She couldn't walk. All she could do was waddle. She was a horrible example of what ten years of living with Aunt Prudence would do to any creature. She looked like a pigmy hippopotamus with hair. Genevieve Trueheart gave Tom a hard time. She followed him. She went wherever he went. She was starved for boys. She never had a chance to meet any in the city. Tom couldn't bend over to tie a boot but her big pink tongue would lick his face. She loved him.

At half-past eight when he finished breakfast and started for school, there on the porch would be Genevieve Trueheart waiting for him.

'She wants to go to school with you, Tommy,' Aunt Prudence always said. 'I think she'd better stay home,' Tom always said, 'It's a mile. That's too far for her.'

'Take poor Genevieve, Tommy,' Aunt Prudence and his mother always said. 'You know how she likes being with you.'

Tom could have said, 'Why should I take her. When I take her the kids at school laugh at me. They ask, "Why don't you send her back to the zoo and get a dog."' But he didn't say that. It would have hurt Aunt Prudence's feelings.

On this morning he thought of something else to say. He said, 'A friend of mine saw a bear on the road. She had two cubs. We'd better leave Genevieve at home. I'll take Rusty.'

'Rusty has to stay to chase pheasants,' his mother said.

'What if I meet a cougar?' Tom said. 'A fat dog like Genevieve would be a fine meal for a cougar.'

'Tommy, stop talking,' his mother said.

'A cougar can pick up a sheep and jump over a fence,' Tommy said.

'Tom Hamilton,' his mother said, 'get to school!'

So Tom Hamilton went down the woodland road with Genevieve Trueheart panting and puffing and snorting behind him. Twice he had to stop while Genevieve sat down and rested. He told her, Rusty doesn't think you're a dog. He thinks you're a great big fat balloon that got a tail and four legs. Tom said, 'Genevieve, I hope a car comes on the wrong side of the road and gets you, you big fat slob.' He never meant it. He said, 'I hope we meet those bears.' He was just talking. He said, 'Do you know what I'm going to do at lunchtime, Genevieve? I'm going to give the fried pork liver that I have for you to another dog, to any dog that looks like a dog and not like a stuffed mattress, and your chocolate, Genevieve, I'll eat it myself.' This was a lie. Tom Hamilton was honest.

Every kid who went to that school came with a dog. Yellow dogs. Brown dogs. Black dogs. White dogs. Black and white dogs. Black, white and yellow dogs. Black, white, yellow and brown dogs. They were a happy collection of dogs, and had long agreed among themselves who could beat whom, who could run faster than whom, who had the most fleas. From nine o'clock in the morning until noon they scratched. From noon until one they looked after their boys. From one until school was out at three they scratched.

These dogs did not welcome Genevieve. They were not jealous because she was a Golden Retriever and had papers to prove it they didn't believe an animal with a shape like Genevieve was a dog. A Mexican hairless dog, one of those small dogs you can slip into your pocket, put his nose against Genevieve's nose, and what did she do, she rolled over on her back with her feet in the air. After that, there wasn't a dog who would have anything to do with Genevieve Trueheart.

The kids ask Tom, 'What's she good for?'

Tom knew the answer but he never told them. She was good for nothing.

'Boy! she's a ball of grease,' the kids said.

'She's a city dog,' Tom said.

'Why don't you leave her at home,' the kids said.

'Because my aunt gives me a dollar a week to walk her to school,' Tom said. A lie.

'Boy, oh, boy!' a kid said, 'I wouldn't be seen with her for two dollars a week.'

After school, Tom waited until all the others had left. He couldn't stand any more unkind words. He took his time going home. He had to. If he hurried Genevieve would sit down and yelp. They came to the woodland road. It was like a tunnel. The tall trees, the Douglas firs, the cedars and the hemlocks, all stretched branches over Tom's head. The air seemed cold even in summer. Owls liked the woodland road, and so did tree-frogs, and deer liked it when flies were after them, but Tom didn't like it much. He was always glad to get out of it and into the sunshine. Often when he walked along this road he had a feeling things were looking at him. He didn't mind Genevieve too much here. She was his company.

This day, Tom knew that something was looking at him. He had the feeling. And there it was!

There it was, all eight feet of it, crouched on a rock, above him, a great golden cat, a cougar, a Vancouver Island panther! It tail was twitching. Its eyes burned green, burned yellow, burned bright. Its ears were flat against its head.

Tom's feet stopped. His blood and all his other juices tinkled into ice, and for a moment the whole world seemed to disappea behind a white wall. A heavy animal brushed against him, and a the shock of that, Tom could see again. It was Genevieve. She had sat down and, to rest herself, was leaning on his leg.

The cougar's ears were still flat, its eyes burning as if lighted candles were in them, it was still crouched on the rock, stil ready to spring.

Tom heard a thump, thump, thump, thump, thump, and he thought it was the sound of his heart, but it wasn't, it was Genevieve beating her tail against the gravel to show how happy she was to be sitting doing nothing. That made Tom mad. If she had been any kind of a dog she would have known about the cougar before Tom did. She should have smelt him. She should have been just out of reach of his claws and barking.

She should have been giving Tom a chance to run away That's what Rusty would have done. But, no, not Genevieve, al she could do was thump her fat tail and look happy.

The cougar came closer. Inch by inch, still in a crouch, he had slid down the rock. Tom could see the movement in his legs He was like a cat after a robin.

Tom felt sick, and cold, but his brain was working. I can't run he thought, if I run he'll be on me. He'll rip Genevieve with one paw and me with the other. Tom thought too, that if he had a match he could rip pages from one of his school books and set them on fire, for he knew that cougars and tigers and leopards and lions were afraid of anything burning. He had no match because supposing his father ever caught him with matches in his pocket during the dry season, then wow and wow and wow! Maybe, he thought, 'if I had a big stone I could stun him'. He looked. There were sharp, flat pieces of granite at the side of the road where somebody had blasted.

The cougar jumped. It was in the air like a huge yellow bird. Tom had no trouble leaving. He ran to the side of the road and picked up a piece of granite.

Of course, when he moved, Genevieve Trueheart, who had been leaning against his leg, fell over. She hadn't seen anything. She lay there. She was happy. She looked like a sack of potatoes.

The cougar walked round Genevieve twice as if he didn't believe it. He couldn't recognise what she was. He paid no attention to Tom Hamilton. He had seen men before. He had never seen anything like Genevieve. He stretched his neck out and sniffed. She must have smelt pretty good because he sat down beside her and licked one of his paws. He was getting ready for dinner. He was thinking, Boy, oh, boy! This is a picnic.

Tom Hamilton could have run away, but he never. He picked up one of those sharp pieces of granite.

The cougar touched Genevieve with the paw he had been licking, friendly-like, just to know how soft the meat was. Genevieve stopped wagging her tail. She must have thought that the cougar's claws didn't feel much like Tom Hamilton's fingers. She lifted her head and looked behind her. There can be no doubt but that she was surprised.

Tom was ashamed of her. 'Get up and fight!' he yelled. Any other dog would fight. Rusty would have put his nips in before the cougar got finished with the job. But not Genevieve. She rolled over on her back and put her four fat feet in the air. She made noises that never had been heard. She didn't use any of her old noises.

The cougar was disgusted with the fuss Genevieve was making. He snarled. His ears went back. Candles shone in his green-yellow eyes. He slapped Genevieve between his paws like a ball.

Tom saw smears of blood on the road and pieces of Genevieve's hide in the cougar's claws. He still had a chance to run away. He never. He threw the piece of granite. He hit the cougar in its middle. The cougar turned, eyes green, eyes yellow.

How long the cougar looked at Tom, Tom will never know.

The sweet smell of Genevieve's chocolate-flavoured blood was too much for the cougar. He batted her about like a ball again. Tom picked up another piece of granite that weighed about ten pounds, and bang! He hit that cougar right in, the face.

The cougar fell on top of Genevieve. Then the cougar stood up and shook its head. Then it walked backwards like a drunken sailor.

And at that moment a bus full of lumberjacks who were going into town rounded the curve. The tyres screeched as the driver stopped it, and thirty big lumberjacks got out yelling like – well, you never heard such yelling, and the cougar quit walking backwards and jumped out of sight between two cedars.

What did Genevieve Trueheart do? That crazy dog waggled on her stomach down the road in the same direction the cougar had gone. She was so scared she didn't know what she was doing.

'Boy, oh, boy! that's some dog,' the lumberjacks said. 'She just won't quit. She's a fighter.'

'Yah!' Tom said.

'She's bleeding,' the lumberjacks said. 'She saved your life. We'd better get her to a doctor.'

They put Genevieve Trueheart and Tom Hamilton in the bus.

'Boy, oh, boy,' the lumberjacks said, 'a fighting dog like that is man's best friend.'

'Yah! Tom said.

The bus went right into Tommy's yard and the thirty lumberjacks told Tommy's mother and father and Aunt Prudence how Genevieve Trueheart, man's best friend, had saved Tommy.

'Yah!' Tommy said.

Then Aunt Prudence put an old blanket and old newspapers over the back seat of her car so that blood wouldn't drip into the fabric when she was taking Genevieve Trueheart to the horse, cow and dog doctor.

Aunt Prudence said, 'Now you know how much she loves you Tommy. She saved your life.'

'Yah!' Tommy said.

Over the Horizon (Galleanez, 1959)

The Girl who never knew Dad

A Head Teacher

As a teacher I was often puzzled as to why one little girl in my class always looked so thoughtful and wistful.

When I told her class they could write an essay on any subject, she wrote under the title *My Dad*.

'I was not born, when my dad died. He was killed two days before Christmas. My mum was putting up the trimmings, when a policeman came to tell her. She took the trimmings down as soon as she had heard what had happened.

'My dad was killed down a pit. Some men were working with him. The roof fell in. The other men ran. My dad could not get away quick enough. He was digging some coal out of the ground, when it happened.

'My dad had promised my mother, brothers and sisters that, as soon as I was old enough, we were going to Zambia.

My dad wanted to work in the mines there. He had planned everything.

'My mum never told me about all this until I was about eight years old. When she told me, I screamed and cried.

'I will always remember my dad. I have a photo of him and I put it under my pillow every night.'

As I read this, I realised how little we teachers in the big schools, coping with large classes, ever know about the children we teach, unless we find out by accident, as I did about this girl.

The Dam

Halliday Sutherland

IN MY TEENS, OUR SUMMER HOLIDAYS WERE SPENT IN THE northern Highlands, and at the age of thirteen I went with my sister, two years my junior, to stay with our granduncle, Robson Mackay, at Olrig Mains, Castleton, near Thurso. He was a retired merchant – a tall, white-bearded old man, and a strict Calvinist. His wife was slim and elderly, always dressed in plain black, with a black lace cap. Her expression was sad, and I cannot recall that she ever smiled.

We arrived in darkness, but the next morning I was out before breakfast to explore the possibilities of the place. By the side of a small bridge on the road a drive went up an incline to the old grey stone house, once a farmhouse. In a little valley on the left of the drive was a 'planting' – a cluster of small pines and bushes. This gave a certain distinction to the place; because on that level windswept soil, trees and hedges are seldom seen, and the fields, like those around Land's End, are hedged with flagstones set on edge.

There were no trees around the house, which stood among grass fields and overlooked a large hayfield in a shallow valley, about a hundred yards wide and a quarter of a mile long. At the foot of the hayfield, and shutting it off from the 'planting,' was a large structure which at first I mistook for a disused railway embankment crossing the valley. In front it was faced with large stones between which grass was growing, and in the centre of the valley it was about twenty feet high. The back of the embankment, three feet wide along the top, was overgrown by thick bushes. Altogether the prospect was not pleasing. There was no sign of a stream, a loch, or a pond, one or other of which was essential to my happiness.

During the forenoon, I discovered at the corner of the hayfield, where the embankment joined the level ground next to the drive, the entrance to a tunnel. It was a square three-foot tunnel, the floor, walls and top being made of paving-stones. Into the tunnel I crept on hands and knees. For the first few yards there was dim light from the entrance, but soon the tunnel turned to the right, and I was in darkness. Somewhere in front of me a rat scuttled away. It was a pity I hadn't had a candle and matches, but no matter; I could creep backwards when I wished to return. I crept on until my head struck an obstacle. My hands discovered this to be a paving-stone, which had fallen from the roof, and was lying diagonally across the tunnel. I could not move the stone, but was able to wriggle over the top of it. Half-way over, hands and head on one side, feet and legs on the other side of the stone, I stopped. It would be difficult to crawl backwards over that obstacle, and I had no room to turn in the tunnel. Discretion was the better part of valour, and I decided to wriggle back. In a moment my jacket was hitched up under my armpits, and I was stuck.

I lay quite still, breathing heavily, and my heart was thumping. It was no use shouting, for no one would hear, and to struggle might make things worse. I must think, but all I could think was that I would die in the tunnel and never be found. No one would think of looking in the tunnel, although whenever a dog was lost the first place one looked for him was in a drain. After a time I saw what seemed to be a glimmer of fight some distance in front. At least I could go on, and the tunnel must come out somewhere. I wriggled forwards, got free of the fallen stone, crept on, turned to the left, and saw daylight. The tunnel emerged in a glade of the 'planting,' behind the embankment. An ideal pirate's lair, with its secret entrance through which I had come. In the middle of the glade was a little stream flowing from a circular brick tunnel at the foot of the embankment. To return to the house I could make my way through the brushwood on the banks of the glade, or through the tunnel. I hesitated. For a pirate there was only one way, and I returned as I had come. Soon the tunnel became quite familiar.

In the afternoon, I explored the hayfield, and found in the centre the rivulet which ran through the circular brick tunnel at the foot of the embankment. At the foot and sides of the entrance to this tunnel was a fixture of grooved iron. The mystery was solved. I was standing at the foot of an unused dam, and the tunnel through which I had crawled was for the overflow. The iron sluice was gone, but a strong wooden board could be made to fit the iron grooves and block the stream. Little did my granduncle know of the possibilities lying at his door – a great loch with trout, boats, and perhaps even a steam launch. It would be a pleasant surprise. The outlook was most promising.

For the next week I cast about for a suitable piece of wood, but large, strong boards were as scarce as trees. For the first few evenings John McCulloch, the village blacksmith, came to the house to give us lessons in woodcarving, my grandaunt's hobby. He was a good-looking young man, with a brown moustache, and of a serious disposition.

In the woodcarving I was not interested, and the wood only served to remind me of the sluice. At last the Devil came to help me, and one morning I entered the smithy. In a corner were a lot of boards, and I had come to buy a board three feet long, two feet five inches wide, and one and a half inches thick.

'What do you want it for?' asked John McCulloch.

'For woodcarving,' I said.

'Well, I'm glad you're taking an interest in the woodcarving. Nothing like it to keep you out of mischief.' He sawed a piece of wood to my measurements, and then planed the edges.

The board slipped easily into the sluice grooves, because I had allowed an inch for expansion when submerged. The edges I greased with lard, and bored a hole below the middle of the upper edge. Through this I passed a strong piece of fencing wire running to the top of the dam, so that if necessary the sluice could be raised. On going down the tunnel I found the rivulet run dry. No water was passing.

The next morning in the hayfield the water in the rivulet was a foot deep. At that rate it would take weeks for the dam to fill, but the time of waiting could be occupied in constructing a raft. I asked one of the sons of the minister, a boy of my own age, if he would like to join me in building a raft. He laughed. 'A raft with no place to sail it, and three miles from the sea!'

'That's all you know,' I said. 'Come with me and I'll show you something.' In the first place I took him down the tunnel, where I now kept a candle and matches, and in the Pirate's Lair swore him to secrecy. He had been born in the district, but the tunnel was a revelation. When I told him what was happening on the other side of the dam, he wished to have nothing to do with it. I pointed out that he had nothing to do with the main project and that no one could blame him for building a raft. I also proposed that the raft be constructed in a field at the back of his house. When the time came a horse could drag it along the road to Olrig Mains. He agreed, and we set off for the manse.

That afternoon rain fell in torrents, and continued all evening and night. As I went to sleep I reflected that the rain, pattering against the window-panes, must be filling the dam. At seven the next morning I awoke and rushed to the window. At first glance I felt unsteady, and then realised the thrill of achievement. It was a wonderful, almost awful sight. In place of the hayfield was a loch with waves on it, and the shore was only twenty yards from the house. At the dam the water was nearly up to the top, and at the other end the loch narrowed into a creek. I dressed and went downstairs. In the hall a maid was unlocking and opening the front door. She also saw the loch and raised her hand above her head. 'Mercy on us!' She turned and ran past me to inform her mistress.

At the dam everything was in order, and the water was swirling down the overflow tunnel, full almost to the top. As soon as the water fell I must go down the tunnel and smash up the dislodged stone lest it should block the waterway. I walked along the top of the dam. Everywhere it felt as steady as a rock. When a dam is going to burst there are premonitory tremblings in the structure, so I had read. But in this dam I could not detect the slightest tremor. I would be able to assure my granduncle at breakfast that there was not the slightest danger.

On the way back to the house I met my granduncle and aunt coming to meet me. The old man leaned on his stick and was trembling with excitement. Both spoke at once: 'Is this your work, boy?'

'It's a mercy your uncle didn't see it first or he might have had a stroke.'

'Yes, Uncle, but it's quite safe,' I answered.

He turned to his wife. 'This mischief must be undone at once. Send for John McCulloch.' With that he went back to the house.

'There's no need, Aunt,' I said, 'to send for John McCulloch. If you want the dam emptied I can do it myself.'

'How did you close the sluice?'

'With a piece of board.'

'Where did you get it?'

'I bought it from John McCulloch.'

'From John McCulloch!' exclaimed my aunt.

'Yes, and I can easily pull it up.'

She went with me to the centre of the dam, where I found the wire and began to pull. The sluice did not move. I pulled harder, the wire slipped through my hands and fell into the water. I sat down and began to take off my shoes.

'What are you going to do now?' she asked.

'Dive for it.'

'You'll do nothing of the kind. You'll be caught in the reeds and drowned. It's bad enough as it is.'

'I won't be drowned. There are no reeds. . . .'

She pointed to the house. 'You march straight back to that house for your breakfast.'

At breakfast there was silence, and at morning family prayers there was no reference in the old man's prayer to the principal event of the day.

After prayers John McCulloch and three men arrived, and crashed their way from the drive through the 'planting' to the Pirate's Lair. I followed at a safe distance and watched their operations. They cut down the largest pine they could find, lopped off the branches, and made the trunk into a pointed battering ram. This they pushed into the circular brick tunnel, and struck the thick end with sledge hammers.

'There's a terrible pressure in there,' said one of the men.

'Yes,' said McCulloch, 'and we must jump when she breaks.'

After a few more blows there was a loud hissing noise.

'That's it, lads!' said McCulloch. 'One or two more.'

After the next blow the battering-ram began to move backwards the men jumped aside, and the largest jet of water I had ever seen shot into the Pirate's Lair, now a roaring torrent on which the pine tree disappeared downstream.

The men departed but I stayed for a time to watch the last entertainment the dam would provide.

From *A Time to Keep*

Going to a Hockey Game with my Sister

Teruko Hyuga

From Japan comes this charming little story. . . .

'TWO IMPORTANT THINGS! ONE: DRESS WARMLY. WEAR A hood or hat, a scarf, gloves, a coat, warm boots. Make sure your head, neck and hands are covered. Two: Go with somebody older. Don't go by yourself. Don't catch cold. It's always very cold over there,' teacher said.

I ran home most of the way from school. A Canadian hockey team was visiting Japan and was going to play against our hometown team, The White Wolf. Mother had promised to take me to watch the game. The White Wolf was once a formidable team in Japan. Nowadays nobody had any hope for the team. Nobody could expect The White Wolf to win. We just wanted to see how well they could defend themselves against the Canadian team.

When I got home, mother was in bed!

'What happened? Are you really sick? Very sick? Of all days, today!' I wailed.

'I'm sorry, Makoto. Soon after you and Asako left for school, I began to feel sick. I had to get into bed. I just can't take you to the game.'

'This is a once-in-a-lifetime event! No Canadian team will come here to Northern Japan again. No foreign team will play against The White Wolf again! The White Wolf will be dead!' I said, almost in tears. 'I have to see this game.'

'Hi,' my sister said, coming in.

'Hi!' Mother's face lit up. 'Asako, you are much older than Makoto. You can take Makoto to the rink, to see The White Wolf team play. I can't go,' mother said in a pleading tone of voice.

My sister is in the ninth grade. I am in the fourth grade. My sister would do. Better than nothing. . . .

'I wish father were alive!' I said sadly.

My sister and I love skating and we are both good skaters, but I am a much better skater, in spite of the age difference. I've been skating since I was three. Actually, I am the fastest skater in the neighbourhood; I have been for years.

Father would have been proud of me and would have taken me to any skating event, no matter what! I thought.

'I have an important test,' my sister said.

'I wish I had a big brother!' I said almost crying. 'I'm sure he'd be happy to take me. He'd love to watch the hockey game, too!'

My sister looked at me.

'Well, today is Saturday. Tonight you can study, and all day tomorrow,' mother said. 'I had promised Makoto. Asako, please take him.'

'All right, but on one condition!'

'Oh,' I grimaced. 'All right. It's such a long way but. . . .'

'It's such a cold day,' mother said.

'Cold or hot, long or short, I can't go by bus!'

'All right. We'll walk. I'm not going to be in the game. It doesn't matter if I'm tired when I get there,' I said reluctantly.

'We'll be warm from walking, ready to watch the game,' my sister said.

My sister gets bus sick, car sick, train sick, all kinds of motion sicknesses!

It's about an hour's walk to the city's natural outdoor rink. Father would have taken me by bus or even by car, I thought as I walked side by side with my sister. Though she is a good skater, my sister isn't interested in hockey games. So, I shouldn't complain . . . She hadn't planned to go to the game. She was going for me.

'Maybe even a stepfather would have been better than nothing,' I said, trying to keep up with my sister.

'I don't know. Though some stepfathers seem nice people,' my sister said. "But we'll never have a stepfather, Makoto.'

'That's for sure. I know,' I sighed.

After all, mother has been a widow all these years. Father died when I was a few months old. But mother has never tried to get married again.

By the time we reached the rink, we felt quite warm though most people looked very cold. There were people all over the place.

The game finally started. Our hometown team was no match for the Canadian team. The White Wolf couldn't make a point. All they did was try to defend themselves against the visiting team. No matter how hard our hometown team tried, the Canadian team scored point after point. It was embarrassing. The White Wolf couldn't score even one point.

My feet were freezing on the ice-covered ground. My gloved hands were freezing in my overcoat pockets. My whole body was freezing! People were stamping their feet to get warm. I did, too. I thought I couldn't stand the cold any longer, many times. But to my surprise, my sister was watching the game excitedly. She was obviously impressed with the Canadian team. I couldn't say I wanted to leave though inside my hood, my head was freezing, too. Biting cold winds were blowing down the snow-covered mountainsides outside our city, near the rink.

To everybody's surprise, after a while, the White Wolf showed astonishing improvement. They still couldn't make a point but they somehow learned how to prevent the Canadian players from making more points. And they never let up. The Canadian team couldn't make another point! Maybe there was still hope for the White Wolf! People around the rink were delighted. When the game was over, everybody was happy in spite of the cold and that the Canadian team won.

Looking frozen, people started leaving the rink for home. They were smiling and talking and proud of the way the White Wolf had proved the team had spirit and courage and could go on.

'So cold!' I said.

I had never been so cold, I thought, as my sister and I started walking. All the other people were heading for the bus stops. All

he bus stops we saw were crowded, and all the buses we saw
vere bulging with people.

In the past, walking warmed me up, but this time I couldn't
get warm. I wasn't sure I'd make it home. I thought I might
freeze to death before I reached home. I was beginning to
worry.

We saw a sweet potato vender. My sister hates sweet potatoes
but she bought five big steaming sweet potatoes and wrapped
each in a paper napkin. She gave me three.

'Put one in each pocket to warm your hands. You can eat
one,' my sister said.

My sister put her hot sweet potatoes into her pockets and
put her hands into the pockets to warm them.

I put two sweet potatoes into my pockets and I ate one
holding it in my shivering hands. I felt a little better. Then I
put my hands in my pockets and held the sweet potatoes. They
warmed my hands.

When I finally saw our house, I was beginning to feel warm
all over – my feet, my hands and my body.

'It was fun, wasn't it?' my sister said.

'Yes!' I smiled.

'Maybe you can join the White Wolf, when you grow up,
and make the team strong again!'

'Yes!' I nodded my head vigorously.

My sister is almost as good as a big brother! I decided.

From *Short Story International*
(Students Series)

Old Warrior

David Walker

The panther launched itself –
a dark shadow of speed and hate

NELL'S FATHER SAT IN ONE ARMCHAIR, HIS MOTHER IN ANOTHER, Neil in the third with his legs under him. The log fire was burning big, and the wet hill air blew in through open windows. The tree frogs were loud outside. Everything was near and sharp and loud. Going away to school tomorrow.

Then the door creaked. Toby ambled straight over to the fireplace, flopped as usual like a ton of bricks, let the bone roll on to the rug, and lay, nose against it. He grunted with satisfaction and drooled a bit at the ripe smell of his prize. It was a high old bone all right.

Mrs Mackenzie had been reading, lost deep in her book. But she sniffed; then erupted with volcanic indignation, 'On my best Bokhara rug! Oh, that stinking animal!'

'He's not stinking! You're st—'

'That'll do,' said Father. 'Remove the offending object.'

Neil removed it between finger and thumb. It was true about Toby being smelly nowadays, but this time it was the bone and not him – both reasons for being angry at Mum.

He took the thing out to the edge of the lawn, got a firmer grip, threw it as far as he could, wiped his hand on the grass, and felt a bit better.

Inside, Major Mackenzie was saying, 'It's a sensitive subject, Celia. Don't you realise the dog means more to him at this moment than you or I or—'

She sighed. 'I know, darling. Have you spoken to him?'

'I will.'

Toby was asleep when Neil came back. Toby was eleven. Toby's father had been a bulldog, his mother a bull terrier. The result was a seventy pounds of muscled ugliness. When he walked through Darjeeling with Neil, ignoring grown-ups but wishing to greet children, he caused alarm among strangers. 'He only wants to say hullo,' Neil often had to explain.

Toby was a famous dog, and a famous fighter when provoked. There was the mastiff which attacked every smaller dog it met.

It made a mistake about Toby. Neither beating, nor pepper, nor water, nor anything else would make him let go of that mastiff's throat. Fortunately, there were dozens of witnesses to say he hadn't started it. Now he was old, dim-sighted, deaf, smelly, and stiff from battle. Age arrives early in India.

Neil thought of everything as he came in and saw his dog asleep. Toby was making dream yelps, which was a funny thing about him because in real life he hunted mute.

'I'm sorry, Neil,' said his mother. 'I didn't mean to say that. He's the best dog in the Himalayas . . . Aren't you, Toby?' But Toby did not hear.

Neil grunted.

'What are you going to do this afternoon?' asked his father.

'I thought I might go for a walk.' Toby was deaf to everything except walks. He woke up.

'Come to the office for a minute, boy.'

Neil followed his father, wondering what it would be this time, and Toby followed Neil. Father shut the door. He went to the window and stared out. 'Going to be more rain,' he muttered. 'This blasted monsoon will never end.' Silence. He turned round. 'Neil, I want to talk to you about Toby.'

Neil looked at the tiger skins and at the snow leopard which was his father's rarest trophy. He knew what was coming. It was what Mr Chatterjee had said last week at the animal hospital. He looked at the Gurkha kukris on the wall. He looked up.

'Yes, father?'

'. . . It's your decision, Neil. Think about it and tell me before you leave tomorrow.'

'Why can't they just be like old people?'

Jim Mackenzie turned again to the window. 'I remember asking my father that once – your grandfather – and he said, because they can't tell us about their aches and pains. One reason, Neil, and a good one. Let me know what you decide.'

'Yes, father.' Neil did not look at Toby.

'Do you want to take the .256 this afternoon in case you see a *karkar*?'

'Oh gosh, yes!' 'Neil's own .22 was too small for deer.'

'Here you are.' His father gave him the Mannlicher carbine from the gun rack, and half a dozen soft-nosed shells. 'No firing at dangerous game; not that you'll see any.'

'O.K. Thanks awfully.' He slung the rifle. It felt good.

Neil put on his jungle boots, slung the old field glasses round his neck, strapped the rolled ground-sheet round his middle, and shouted good-bye to mum.

She came to the door. 'Well,' she said, being silly, 'if it isn't Jim Corbett himself. What are you hunting today, colonel?'

'I'm going after a barking deer,' Neil said, ignoring that crack about Jim Corbett, the tiger hunter. But his mother's face changed. It never stayed the same for long, and now he saw it change to wanting to come with him. He might have offered to take her, because she was what father called 'a good jungle woman,' but he didn't. 'See you later,' he said.

'Be back by six, darling. And please stick to the paths. I heard that panther twice last night.' She made a harsh pantherish rasp exactly right, and laughed, and looked rather sad again. 'The house is going to be so quiet after tomorrow.'

He escaped. Toby gave one deep woof, and gambolled about like his old bouncing self, or his young self, as he always did for a minute at the beginning of a walk. Then he sobered down to a double limp from the mastiff wound on his right shoulder and a panther swipe on his left quarter.

I wonder if Sher Bahadur could come? Neil thought. So he went by the weighing shed. Sher Bahadur had been his father's orderly in the Gurkhas. He was a square, short man, just about as broad as he was long. He sprang to his feet and quivered into a superb salute. 'General Sahib! 'It was an ancient joke and still funny.'

'Oh, great brave tiger Sher Bahadur, and chopper of many heads by night,' said Neil in Nepalese, 'can you come hunting?'

'Not this baby, Nee-ul,' said Sher Bahadur. He had picked up that one in the Italian campaign and was proud of it, almost his entire spoken English vocabulary, although he could understand a bit. 'There is a dangerous Major Mackenzie in these hills who orders that I weigh tea this afternoon.'

Toby had come over to say hullo. He ignored non-family adults, but Sher Bahadur was a friend of many walks. He patted Toby once on the head. 'Old Warrior.'

Neil told him what his father had said. He couldn't have talked about it to anybody else. 'I have to decide.'

'You are a man, Nee-ul, and you will decide.'

'Come on, Toby. He wasn't a man, and he didn't want to decide.'

They left the buildings and followed a path through trees. The hillside was bursting green with growth. You could hear a seeping trickle of water everywhere under the cicadas trilling 'rain' more loudly now than ever. Three months' rain, a hundred inches, and more to come before the monsoon rolled back in October. The mist had thinned to wisps of cloud climbing out of the valleys. Far away south and six thousand feet down, there was sunshine on the plains, a different, sticky world.

Neil and Toby came to terraced slopes where tea bushes were dark green and the hill women were picking green tips and chattering nineteen to the dozen while their fingers flew at the work. He quickened pace because lately they seemed to stare and giggle and make remarks.

Somebody did now. 'Aaaiii!' she called. 'See the beautiful boy, sahib!' Which was quite embarrassing, and meant for his ears. They knew he understood the hill tongue as well as they did. Cackles of laughter.

'So many fat, lazy old cows mooing!' he said loudly. It was a great success.

He reached the end of the tea garden. The country beyond was too steep for cultivation. The path swung into the head of a gully where the stream gathered, and out round the next shoulder.

Neil stopped to look back at the red-roofed house and buildings. You never thought much about home until there was only a week to go. Then it was the last day suddenly. And after Christmas you were going to school in England.

'Good boy, Toby,' he said. 'We'll have a rest in a minute.' Toby wagged his tail. He was wheezing. There were no level walks, but this was the easiest one. They crossed the shoulder.

Neil unrolled the groundsheet. It was father's, from the war, too noisy a thing for stalking, but waterproof and very good for wearing when you sat still because of the blotched brown and green camouflage.

He did not wear it now, but sat on one half and put Toby on the other. The hillside dropped off almost vertically for a few hundred feet; farther down there were trees again, and ferns among the rocks, and lush green grass. Somewhere out beyond all that, two hill men were having an across-the-valley conversation, voices pitched high; they might be five miles from here. But the sounds of home, which was only just round the corner, were cut off completely.

Neil watched. There were many tints of green, brown, grey; some of the wet rocks were black. Nothing was the colour he wanted – the russet red of a karkar, the barking deer that lurked so daintily in shaded places. He would have had a much better chance lower down, but this was Toby's walk, and Toby was not able. Toby snoozed.

Neil spied through the glasses for a while, searching clump by clump methodically, but nothing doing. 'Monkeys,' he said, putting his hand on the dog's square head. Toby did not have the cramped, shallow skull of a modern bull terrier. He had a head on him, ugly though it was. At the word 'monkeys' he opened his right eye in the centre of its black patch, and rumbled. Toby had it in for monkeys, particularly for the big grey langur males who had it in for him. These now were langurs, too far away for the dog to see. They swung through trees and over the ridge. After that, a party of minivets flashed across, the males bright scarlet, the females yellow. Neil had a good feeling of birds and beasts and him and Toby. It was time to go on.

They came to a sandy ravine. There were pug marks and the tracks of lesser game.

'Toby!' he said loudly. 'Want to go on? You old fool, Toby.' Calling him an old fool was the way to make Toby smile. He did now – a hideous, disreputable leer before he rolled on ahead. The path swung into the next cascading stream, wound out to the next spur or shoulder: the teeth of a giant lumberman's saw – it was that kind of hill country.

Toby led. He could decide for himself how far he wanted to walk. That, anyway, could be Toby's decision. They went through loud water, and now were following the shoulder. The air was damp and thin and cool. Clouds were piling in, grey again. The distant plains were not visible.

Toby's head had been low, but suddenly it came up; the skin wrinkled on his shoulders; he sniffed. Then he gave a whimper, quite an insignificant noise. He made it only when he caught a hateful scent – monkey or panther or bear or pig.

'Steady, boy,' said Neil, putting him on the leash. Nowadays he ran into things and hurt himself.

The dog pulled hard. He was still tremendously strong. 'I wonder if I should turn back.' Thought Neil. Then he thought, perhaps this is our last time, and it'll only be some old monkey scent; he'll quieten down in a minute. But he unsung the carbine and held it in his right hand.

Toby did not quieten down. The hackles bristled dark all along his back, and he took charge, blundering along the path. It narrowed from three feet to two feet to one foot, and there was the point of the shoulder now.

'Stop, Toby!' Toby heard, and eased a little.

Neil knew this place. You crossed the shoulder, and then for twenty yards or so, as you swung in again, you were not on a path, but on a ledge below a vertical cliff, above steep scree. They would stop there to have a last spy for karkar and then turn home. Toby whimpered again, but was well in hand as they reached the apex of the spur. They turned.

It was not old monkey scent. At the far end of the ledge stood a panther.

A great many things flashed across Neil's mind in that second. Too narrow for the brute to turn. Too steep for it to climb. Could come on. Might break down the scree. Himself with leash in one hand, carbine in the other. Had to hold Toby. Horrible, slender, wicked panther . . . .

He was hauling his hardest on Toby when the panther crouched, tail switching, coiled to—

Toby attacked, tearing the leash from Neil's fingers. As Neil stumbled forward, he watched his dog hurl himself along the ledge, bunched bone and muscle, silent but for scrabbling claws.

The hill panther had hunted and killed many dogs for its favourite meat. But it had never seen a dog like this, a dingy white monstrosity with one black eye, a braver fighter than it was itself. The panther charged also – a hundred and forty pounds against seventy. The cat snarling, the dog mutes. They met in a thudding fury of fangs and claws; then the two twisting, contrasted bodies rolled over the edge and down the scree.

Neil watched them go – writhing, tangled, the dog at the panther's throat – heads over tails in a showering rattle of loose stones. He dared not fire. But a moment later he realised that he should have risked the shot, because there could be only one end to this. However, brave Toby was and, however, firm his throat-hold, the panther would break him.

But Neil was too late. He saw it happen before they reached the bottom of the scree. The pale body swung out and away from the tawny body, and the cat had the space it needed. Fore-paw smacked hindquarters. It was a vicious stroke, nearly too fast to see. Toby's jaw-grip was loosening already as they tumbled out of sight into green undergrowth.

Silence. Only the drip-drip of water and the eternal tree frogs. No movement at all below. Neil ran down the moving scree, stumbled, recovered, slithered to the bottom. He shouted. It was a cracked imitation of a shout to scare the panther. Then he was into bushes, ferns, grass, thorns, carbine at his waist, forcing a passage down. Now a rustling clump of bamboo, but no white Toby, no deadly panther.

'My fault,' he thought. 'All my fault.' His coat was torn, his face scratched, his body soaked. He went on. Was that –?

No, it was not the crouching leopard. It was a dappled rock. And that flicker of white was not old Toby. It was a paradise flycatcher, flitting away with streamer tails.

Then he saw Toby. His dog lay at the edge of the stream. Toby was alive with a broken back and many wounds. He was only just alive, but he knew Neil's hand. He opened both eyes.

'Oh, Toby.' It could not be long.

Toby growled. 'I smell you, enemy,' he growled. There was another noise above the tiny splashing of the stream. It came from higher up. It was the panther swaying long grass, a bold hill panther with a sore throat, wanting its kill.

Neil held the rifle in his shoulder. He was not afraid, although his heart thumped fast. Father had said, 'Never take on a panther in closed country. Never!' And this was an angry panther.

There was movement in the grass again from right to left. It might come straight or it might cross that open patch of rock to complete the circle. They generally circled first, didn't they? Neil had not shot a panther, but he had read every big-game book he could find.

The panther did not come straight. It crossed the ten yards of rock in two galloping strides.

Neil fired, saw the hindquarters slew slightly, heard it grunt. Then it was out of sight behind that clump of bamboo. He had hit it, he thought, but he knew the shot was too far back, probably a flesh wound. The brute had not even stumbled.

He looked down.

'Poor Toby,' he said. 'Poor boy, I'm sorry, Toby.'

Neil did not have time to think about Toby's death, for the panther growled from the bamboos. And it was not thinking but feeling that said, 'You're not going to eat my dog. You killed him and I'm going to kill you.'

But then Neil did think; he thought fast. Could he put Toby's body on his back and climb the other side of the gully where it was open ground for a shot? No, too heavy and too steep. A tree? Yes, there was a tree beside him, gnarled and small, but with a fork low down. Climb it and leave Toby where he was? But if you missed, the panther would take the dog and be gone in a flash.

Neil had made his plan. He began to carry out the plan now without ever taking his eyes off those bamboos where the panther growled again. He loosed the belt which held his groundsheet, undid the cords, unrolled it on the steep ground, spread it wide, hauled the body, still limp, on to the centre. Then his heart jumped because the bamboo fronds were moving. But it was only the monsoon deluge beginning again, pattering on his groundsheet, on leaves overhead, drowning lesser noises.

All this Neil had done with one hand. Now he laid down the .256, gathered the corners of the groundsheet, tied them with the cord, making a sack for old Toby. Would it come now? If it has any sense it'll come now, he thought in a standing-outside-himself sort of way.

But the panther did not come. Now Neil had the belt fixed, too, and buckled round his neck. He picked up the rifle, staggered to his feet, and tried to clamber into that fork. He tried desperately in the loud rain, but he was not strong enough.

Down again, belt over his head. What a clever idea about the groundsheet sack, and what a waste of time. He took seventy pounds dead weight in his arms and managed to raise it to the fork. Then he climbed above, wedged himself, heaved, steadied it again.

Bit by bit, Neil dragged his own body and Toby's body higher. It was an easy tree to climb, the kind of tree you pretty well ran up when you heard game moving and wanted to spy. But it was not easy now.

He rested. Legs, arms, stomach, lungs all ached, and the lights of exhaustion flashed. His hand, grasping at a green, slimy bough, trembled like some old man's. The rain fell in a drenching, solid wall of noise. But gradually his breathing slowed, the shakes and aches lessened, heat dwindled into the middle of his body. No panther.

He was ten or twelve feet up the tree. The camouflaged sack that was Toby, or had been Toby, hung from a branch stump just below him. It was secure. Neil was secure enough himself that is, he was wedged so as not to fall out. But he knew that he could be pulled out. The panther could get at him with a jump or it could get at him by climbing. 'I should just have slipped away,' he thought. 'What difference would it make, when Toby was dead already? Slipped away? No, sneaked away after letting him be killed for me. I never even did anything. I just let it happen.'

Neil watched the clump of bamboo. It was about on a level with his own head. No movement at all. Was the panther still there? Had it moved down left to take him from behind? Had it gone altogether? Behind! Yes, that was what the shivers in his spine said. He whipped his head round. No panther.

And now the light was fading, and every dancing leaf or blade could be dancing from rain or from a long slinking body. That sound! But there was no sound anywhere except rain.

Neil began to shiver again -- this time from cold, and because he was afraid. As he shifted position, the panther growled. It was in the same place still. It was waiting for the dusk that was not far off.

Not knowing had been the bad thing. He stopped being afraid. He had the sights aligned just this side and below, finger on the trigger. If only it would show itself. If he could just get a glimpse of where the head was.

But the panther did not move. He knew that when the time came for it to move, it would not stroll in a lord-of-the-jungle way as a tiger would stroll. It was a panther, and it had been touched up by a bull terrier at the throat and by a bullet somewhere far back. That growl had said, 'I'm going to get you.' It would kill for its dog meat.

Neil should have been feeling sad about Toby, but suddenly he was rather happy in a calm, murderous kind of way. He had never felt like that before. 'You're wrong, you stinking panther. I'm the one who's going to get you.'

It was much darker. He looked at his watch. Six-twenty. 'Be back by six, darling,' she had said, and it was a grey, wet, early night, and she would be in an awful stew already, particularly if they'd heard the shot. They might not have.

'Don't imagine horrors, my love,' father would be telling her. He treated her as a joke when she got fussed, which was quite clever of him, although she was much cleverer than he was. What's father going to say when I get home? If I get. . . .

Neil watched. He took his left hand off for a moment to wipe the rain out of his eyes. He heard an owl scream along the hill, and jackals howling far down in the deep valley. Otherwise rain. He was very cold. What would happen if the panther did not come? Was that voices?

Just then lights appeared. They came round the shoulder where he and Toby had met the panther, and men were shouting. They were quite close.

'Neil!' in father's loud bellow, and 'Nee-ul!' from Sher Bahadur.

Neil did not answer. He was watching the bamboos. They were indistinct. He could not make out one slim shoot from another, but something was happening there.

'Neil!'

'Nee-ul!'

'Shut up,' he said under his breath as the panther launched itself, a dark, long shadow of speed and hate. His bullet flame stabbed. Reload. Hit.Panther below, not dead, very much alive. Neil swung round, straining himself to get the barrel down. He saw it crouched there, head back, snarling.

Then it climbed, paws on either side of the trunk, clawing. Like a house cat climbing from a dog, he thought in the galloping moment. But this was climbing to, not from. He fired. It came on. Eyes vertical slits. Reloaded. Stink of breath was hitting him as he fired yet again into the panther's face. It did not climb the last two feet. It stayed where it was. Then the devilish energy slackened. Neil saw that happen. He saw his panther slide down, claws rasping, strike the first fork, and roll back dead.

'Neil!'

He could hear them on the scree. He should answer now, but coldness and weakness were everywhere, and deep.

Father with his big rifle, Sher Bahadur with the five-celled torch. Men carrying lanterns. The light shone on the dead panther then up to the groundsheet sack, then blinded Neil.

'What the hell's all this?' Father did not sound pleased or relieved. He sounded red-hot angry, and when father was angry, which hardly ever happened, then the whole shooting match exploded. 'Didn't I tell you—'

'Major Sahib!' Sher Bahadur said. 'See!' The beam was on Toby's shroud dangling from its branch.

'What happened?'

Neil told it. He could not say much. He was just realising what he had done to Toby. 'The panther broke his back, and it was all my fault, and I—'

'Well, I'll be darned,' Jim Mackenzie muttered at the end. 'Help the boy down, Sher Bahadur.'

Neil got down all right, but as soon as he reached the ground something went wrong. He couldn't help it. He just couldn't.

'Steady now, old fellow,' father said after a while. Tears made him feel awkward.

'A man who is a man may weep,' said Sher Bahadur.

But Neil stopped crying.

'Drink this, Neil.' He drank the burning stuff from a flask and choked. The heat went through him. The coolies cut a pole to carry the panther.

'Take the rifles, Sher Bahadur. I'll carry old Toby.'

Which his father did, and they climbed past bamboos sounding in the rain and up sliding scree, and here was the ledge where Toby had killed himself for you, and on towards home.

Father stopped in the darkness. 'Are you all right, Neil?'

'Yes.' Neil was warmer again, but he was not all right.

Jim Mackenzie did not always understand his moody, hotheaded son; he understood now. 'Sher Bahadur,' he said in Nepalese. 'Oh, brother! Did Toby die well?'

'As one brave soldier for another,' said Sher Bahadur. 'And few old warriors may die thus.'

Argosy, December 1959

The Phantom Pirates

Rick Ferreira

Two boys in search of adventure meet with the legendary pirates of the West Indies. A spooky tale from Trinidad and Tobago. . . .

EVERY STUDENT ON TOBAGO KNEW THE LEGEND OF CAPTAIN Skull and his band of bloodthirsty pirates.

It told how once, about two centuries ago, Tobago had been the Captain's favorite island in the West Indies. With its sheltered bay, it provided a safe place for him to hide his ship . . . then, unmolested, the pirates could bury their stolen treasure, deep in the white sand of the beach, just beyond the tumbling blue waves of the Caribbean Sea.

The Captain himself had been a fearsome sight to behold!

Over his head he always wore a black hood. On it there had been the outline and features of a grinning skull, painted white, with the Captain's crazed black eyes gleaming through the eye-slits. . . .

So ran the legend.

Christopher and Jonah had heard it all ever since they could remember. And the other part, too – the part that the boys had always scoffed at – that on the first night of each full moon, Captain Skull and his crew returned to the beach to dig up their treasure chests, then to check by moonlight the gold and silver coins, the gem-stones and the pearls, big as a pigeon's eggs. And they were furious if their treasure had been disturbed. Apparently, if there was one thing Captain Skull and his pirates couldn't stand, it was thieves!

Tonight, with the gigantic full moon riding high and clear above the sea and the coconut palms, Christopher and Jonah had decided that the time had come to investigate the old legend, once and for all. They both felt brave enough and, anyway, it was just an old island tale. . . .

But when the big alarm clock with the double copper bells woke them up with its racket, it was well after midnight. So the boys argued breathlessly, racing along in the moonlight, heading for the clump of coconut trees and the winding path that led steeply down to the beach.

'You set that clock, not me,' Jonah protested.

'Hold it, Masta Chris. . . I drop my piece of sugarcane!' Jonah's thin legs braked to a halt while his eyes searched the ground, almost day-bright by the light of the moon.

'How can you think of chewing sugarcane now?' And Christopher's pyjama clad legs kept on racing. 'We're already too late. See you on the beach, glutton!'

'Found it!' Jonah cried, hitching up the old shorts he slept in. Then he was back in his stride, racing after Christopher.

Being twelve-year-old was the only thing the boys had in common. Blonde, chubby Christopher was English, and Tobago had been his adopted home since he was two and his widowed father had taken up the post of Medical Superintendent on the island. Jonah was a native, and he was shiny black and a compulsive eater. But he was still the thinnest twelve-year-old in Tobago.

The boys raced on through the warm night, through the sad signing of the coconut trees, and the sound of the sea grew louder as they came nearer. They reached the headland together, breathless and gasping, with Jonah sucking noisily away on his stick of sugarcane. They were just about to plunge down the familiar steep path to the beach, when they stopped. Utterly frozen – like two gilded statues in the moonlight – they stood, while their eyes stared unblinking at the scene on the beach below.

For the pirates were there!

Toiling away just beyond the reach of the waves, and buffeted by the winds from the sea, some were bending over a vast sea chest, it's heavy lid thrown back, while they checked its precious contents. A dozen others were using wide shovels to flatten another section of the beach . . . where presumably, another chest had been checked and reburied. They seemed surly and suspicious -- and looked smelly, too, Christopher thought – and all were busy.

All but Captain Skull.

He was standing guard, with a hand on the head of his cutlass and a murderous-looking pistol leveled at his men. And Captain Skull looked exactly as the boys had imagined he would. Except in just one terrifying detail. Even from the height where they stood, Christopher and Jonah could see that the Captain's head was no longer hidden by the black hood with the skull bones painted in white. Christopher's teeth started rattling like a bag of marbles, and Jonah choked on his stick of sugarcane.

For now, Captain Skull truly deserved his name. His head was a real, grinning skull of white, bleached bones!

At that very moment the skull swung up and away from the beach, searching out the two boys bathed in moonlight, high up on the headland.

Christopher and Jonah stood, helpless and unmoving, while the gaping eye sockets of Captain Skull stand trained on them, like a deadly double barreled shotgun. Then they watched the grinning jaws swing open. . . .

'Blasted spies!' the Captain roared. 'Up above, lads!'

With his cry, a hurricane of sound came rushing up from the beach: the clang of spades thrown hastily down, the thud of sea-boots pounding across the sand. Then the pirates were jostling and pushing and swearing . . . all anxious to scramble up the steep path to the headland and capture the boys. Captain Skull pointed with the cutlass he had drawn from his waistband, and the moonlight that filled his eye sockets glinted wickedly on the naked blade.

'Up there! We need cabin boys! Get 'em both!'

But life and motion had come back to Christopher and Jonah. A second later they had turned and were running with the speed only terror can inspire. Back through the coconut trees they raced, back along the beach road, then down the long rough lane that led to the bungalow.

They ducked under the verandah rail, then their bare feet were slapping the wooden floor as they sped for the safety of their bedroom. Then they were in the bedroom, with the door slammed shut. Christopher tumbled headlong into his bed, and Jonah made a flying leap for the rope hammock he slept in.

And Jonah promptly fell out. He lay on the floor and laughed, slightly hysterical and filled with relief. Christopher sat up in bed and laughed, too. But it was quite a while before the boys could fall asleep again.

Salome woke them by throwing open the wooden shutters, and the sunlight poured into the bedroom like yellow paint from a can. Salome was Jonah's mother. She was also housekeeper to Christopher and his father, and she ran the bungalow with bustling good humor. And great firmness.

She was firm now.

'Why you two boys sleep so late? You talk and talk all night, I'll bet. Up, Masta Chris! Your Dad staying at the hospital for the next two nights and he said you better be good!' She trundled over to Jonah's hammock and shook it with a massive arm. 'Out of that hammock, lazybones! And Jonah, see you feed the hens before breakfast. . . .' Then Salome was gone and the wooden floor of the bedroom stopped its alarming creaking.

The boys never disobeyed Salome.

Ten minutes later, Jonah was throwing corn to a bunch of clucking hens, and Christopher was walking on the very beach where Captain Skull and his pirates had been so busy last night. In the bright sunshine, Christopher felt none of the blind terror that had made him and Jonah race so madly back to the bungalow.

And then he saw the coin.

It was a fat, round, gold coin, glinting in the morning sun, and lying next to a dried branch from a coconut tree. Christopher broke into a run, his blue eyes wide with surprise and delight.

'Whoopee!' he yelled as he scooped the coin up from the sand. And though the sand was already warm, the coin felt heavy and cold, but Christopher hardly noticed that. He clutched it so tightly that his fist ached, as he raced back across the sand and scrambled up the path to the headland.

He was completely winded when he found Jonah at the rear of the bungalow, shooing half a dozen hens back into the hen house. 'All going to lay eggs today,' Jonah said with satisfaction. The thought of anything edible always gave Jonah a warm, secure feeling. 'You look excited. What's up?'

Christopher took a deep breath, then he opened his right hand. It was a great, dramatic moment. 'Look, Jonah! Look. . . .'

Jonah looked. Jonah swallowed very loudly and took a step backwards. 'That there is pirate gold! The good Lord protect you now. . . .'

'Me? Gosh! Oh, Jonah . . . I – I forgot! I was so excited.'

'But you crazy? Like me, you know the other part of the story . . . never pick up pirate money from the beach. You know that the dead pirates will come to you now to get their coin. What'll you do then?' Fearful though he was, Jonah found that he was rather enjoying himself. 'And no good you taking it back to the beach, either. You picked it up . . . now they must punish you!'

Christopher listened, aghast. 'You – you think they'll come – tonight?'

'Sure as dark!' Jonah said, then he remembered that Christopher was his friend. His best friend. 'Say! Why don't we go see Mister Hippy Harry right now? No – after breakfast! But you say nothing to my ma about your pirate money. She want to put gold on all her teeth. Any gold. Even pirate money gold!'

Christopher managed a wan smile.

He knew all about Salome's obsession to cover every tooth with a thin gold cap. Her wide smile was already half gold. 'Hippy Harry will know what to do, won't he, Jonah? He's so clever. He knows almost everything. What do you think?'

'I think . . . when he knows you are in mortal danger, he'll help.' That sounded very reassuring, until Jonah ruined it all by saying: 'We got fried pork for breakfast . . . just you smell!'

And at that moment Salome's great head came out of the kitchen window, and the sunlight caught the gold caps already in her mouth. 'You boys come in now. It's ready.'

Jonah put a wiry arm around Christopher's shoulder. 'Anything you don't want . . . you just put on my plate, O.K.?'

'O.K.,' Christopher said gloomily. 'But how you can think of your belly at a time like this, I just don't know. . . .'

The sun was a hot blaze in the sky when they finally got to Hippy Harry's shack, high in the hills above the town. The shack looked a part of the fern-covered hillside, as if it had grown out of the soil. It was ramshackle and wooden, with a thatched roof of coconut branches. It nestled deep in a small forest of towering bamboo trees.

It looked spooky even in brilliant sunlight.

'Masta Chris . . . you go on in and tell about the gold money. I'll just climb the mango tree at the back and bring you in '

'No you don't! Christopher grabbed hold of Jonah's thin arm, and together the two boys walked between the rows of giant sunflower trees up to the half-open door.

Inside they found Hippy Harry.

The middle-aged Englishman was tanned to a deep coppery color and he wore his thinning black hair half way down his back. Long ago he had settled for the slow, contented way of life on

Tobago, but only in the last few years had 'Mister Harry' become 'Mister Hippy Harry.' It was all the same to him.

The shack was filled with books and shells, fishing rods and piles of old newspapers – and hens. For Hippy Harry kept them, too. Except that he allowed them to cluck their way in and out the back door, to flap onto every surface, scratching away happily and unnoticed. Except when there were visitors.

'Come on!' Hippy Harry shouted now. 'Out you go!'

He swept two hens to the floor from the long wooden table and made room for his bare elbows among the unwashed enamel plates. 'Is it raining outside? You two look like orphans of the storm. Never saw such long faces.' He gave a huge sigh and cupped his stubbly chin. 'All right, let's have the story, boys. . . .'

Christopher told him the events of last night – and the morning. Finally, he took the fat gold coin from the pocket of his jeans and laid it down before Hippy Harry.

They all looked at it for a while in awed silence.

At last Hippy Harry uncapped his chin and touched the coin with a finger that was none too clean. 'Right! Know what it is? Well, it's a Spanish doubloon. Old Spanish money . . . couple of centuries old. Christopher! Picking it up was bad enough, but running away with it. . . .' The long hair swished on his back as Hippy Harry shook his head. 'That's bad. Very bad!'

'But I was excited. I – I clean forgot all about that part of the story.' Christopher couldn't help feeling annoyed that nobody understood his shock and delight on the beach. 'Even Jonah would have done the same—'

'Not me! This boy's got brains.'

'Simmer down, you two. Well, the thing is . . . just how do we frighten them off when they come back to reclaim the doubloon? They'll do it tonight. The moon will still be full.'

'We thought they would,' Christopher said, gulping.

'He in mortal danger, Mista Harry!' Jonah echoed. Jonah quite liked the phrase. He also liked the look of a bunch of bananas dangling from a low roof-beam. He tried hard to put the bananas out of his mind. 'But I sleep in his room and I don't think it is that easy. You ask Masta Chris.'

'Jonah is awfully brave—' Christopher began loyally, but Hippy Harry cried: 'I've got it! They all died on the gallows – every black hearted rogue. You do know that hanging was the punishment for piracy on the high seas, don't you boys?' Hippy Harry slapped an open palm on the pile of old newspapers on the rickety table. His sharp blue eyes swung from one boy's face to the other. 'I'm going to rig up a miniature gallows -- with crossarm, dangling noose, and so on. All in bamboo and wood. Then you put the model over your bed, Chris . . . and they will take fright instead. It's like showing a crucifix to a vampire. You'll have 'em out of your room before you can say "pieces of eight".'

Hippy Harry grinned cheerfully at both of them -- as his left hand slid the coin smoothly from sight under the pile of old newspapers.

Well, boys, I must get to work. I'll have your little charm ready in about an hour. What will you two do in the meantime?'

Jonah had the answer.

'We get us a few ripe mangoes!' he said promptly, and Christopher gave him a quick glance to see if he, too, had seen what Hippy Harry had done with the coin. But Jonah's mind was firmly on food. 'Ain't it ripe time for guavas, too? How much can we eat, Mista Harry?'

'All you can hold!' And Hippy Harry waved cheerfully, then disappeared into the back room of the shack.

'Glutton!' Christopher said, wandering over to the single window. There was a very fat goat eating the lower leaves of the sunflower trees, and he watched with interest.

But he turned from the window when Jonah said: 'Now, boy – no need to get shaky at the knees!' And Christopher laughed, for Jonah was now seated at the rickety table, doing a very good imitation of Hippy Harry. With a hand on the pile of old newspapers, Jonah grinned, than he nodded wisely, 'You come to the right place, Christopher. Them ghost pirates are in mortal danger now . . .'

'And how about those sweet, sweet mangoes?' Christopher asked. He knew that the mere mention of fruit would get his friend out of the chair, through the back door and up the nearest tree.

And it did.

The boys climbed and ate and laughed for more than an hour. They forgot all about the coming night and its possible terrors. Then Hippy Harry called them back out of the bright heat into the cool dimness of the shack.

'Well, boys . . . what do you think of it?'

Christopher and Jonah looked at the model gallows in silence. It looked both crude and toy-like and yet, somehow, very real indeed. The thick cord that dangled from the arm of the gallows was pulled into a tight noose. And with his neck in the tight noose was the rigid figure of a pirate.

'The figure came from a toy kit I bought last year. It adds that last finishing touch.' Hippy Harry gazed proudly at his handiwork. 'It'll do the trick, boys. You'll see. Now, have you got any kind of shelf above your bed, Chris?'

Christopher nodded, his eyes still glued to the frightful model.

'Jonah, is there a big battery torch up at the bungalow?'

It was Jonah's turn to nod.

'Good,' said Hippy Harry. 'Well, when they come, and Chris here starts yelling – that will be your cue, Jonah. You turn your torch on that shelf and keep it steady. They'll simply melt away at the sight of the gallows. Just take my word for it.'

The two boys sighed in unison. Then Jonah said: 'You can carry my mangoes, Masta Chris. I'll hold that – that thing. . . .'

Christopher gulped. He suddenly felt very grateful for having a friend as brave as Jonah. They said their goodbyes to Hippy Harry and went back out into the blaze of the noonday sun.

They reached the bungalow in the early afternoon and spent the hours till dark trying to avoid Salome. But they couldn't avoid her forever. At early supper, just before sunset, she said to Christopher: 'You hear me, Masta Chris? Why you no eating your fried breadfruit? You always saying you like fried breadfruit—'

'He got troubles,' Jonah cut in. 'But I'll have his piece, ma, after I finish mine.' All the same, Christopher noticed that Jonah, too, was off his food – for once.

'You two keep stuffing your bellies with ripe mangoes. . .' Salome grumbled when she finally took their plates back to the kitchen.

Then the boys sat silent, watching the huge sun stain land and sky a deep crimson, then very slowly drop into the sea without making even a tiny splash. They stayed silent as the tropic night came alive . . . the frogs croaked, the fireflies winked and glowed and the mosquitoes came whining out of the star-filled dark.

They sat on, smacking at the mosquitoes for a while longer.

'We'd better go in,' Christopher said reluctantly. 'I heard Salome go down to her cottage. I do wish that your mother would sleep in the house. Especially tonight.'

'Ma likes her own place, you know that. Anyways, then pirates will be after her gold teeth the moment she opens her mouth to scream.'

That made Christopher laugh, but Jonah didn't even smile at his own joke.

'Stop worrying, Jonah,' said Christopher. 'We'll be all right with the gallows thing. In fact, I don't think that they will come here at all.' Christopher tried to sound offhand and mysterious, both at the same time. 'They just might call on someone else we know, instead.'

But Jonah didn't seem to hear any of it, for he just said: 'I sleep in the hammock, eh?'

'Well,' Christopher said, 'if you'd rather come into my bed. . . .'

'With the thing over my head?' Jonah grinned then. 'No, it's the hammock for me. And the big torch.'

They took a long time to fall asleep.

Yet they finally did, lulled by the faraway sound of the sea and the wind in the coconut trees. Then, much later – and very slowly – a huge moon climbed into the night sky, and its light split through the wooden shutters of the room where the boys were mow soundly sleeping.

And on the stroke of midnight the pirates came.

Suddenly they filled the room, clear and sharp to see, yet ghostly and untouchable as the moonlight. They swore and shouted, banged their pistols on the walls and the wooden shutters, slapped their cutlasses on the foot of Christopher's bed. . . .

'Wake up, laddie. The gold!'

'We'll have the coin back. . . .'

'Cap'n, slit his thiefin' throat!'

And a moment later, the pirates made way for Captain Skull.

Slowly he advanced on Christopher until his fleshless head was just inches away and the empty eye sockets were two deep pools of evil. The lower jaw swung down as the Captain made ready to speak.

It was too much for Christopher. 'I haven't got it,' he wailed. 'I haven't got the coin! Jonah! The torch. . . .'

From the madly swinging hammock came a sudden beam of light. It went clean through the pirates like a bright sword blade – and straight into Christopher's eyes.

'On the shelf, Jonah! The shelf. . . .'

But now the hammock was swinging more violently than ever. Then Jonah fell out of the hammock and hit the wooden floor with a thud, and the torch rolled away, spilling a line of brilliant light.

His jaws clinking and clattering, Captain Skull roared: 'It's the little blackamoor! He has the doubloon!' The Captain had turned away from Christopher, and now the eyeless sockets and one skeleton hand were all pointing squarely at Jonah.

The pirates had gone silent for a moment, but now they again erupted into shouted oaths and threats.

'I'll have your liver for breakfast!'

'Give the gold over. . . .'

'You'll walk the plank!'

Jonah came shakily to his feet, then he threw something high into the roof. 'Take it then,' Jonah shouted, half sobbing. 'I wanted the gold for ma. I never gave her anything before!'

A dozen unwashed faces were upturned, a dozen pairs of red-rimmed eyes watched the coin spin in the moonlight . . . then a huge skeleton hand shot up and caught it in midair. And at that exact moment, Captain Skull and his pirates vanished. In a split second the room held only the moonlight and the two shaking boys.

In the sudden silence, Jonah swallowed the other half of his sob.

'Jonah. . . ?' Christopher shook his head in bewilderment. 'How did you get the coin? I saw Hippy Harry steal it!'

'Me, too.' Jonah came over to the bed and took a deep breath. 'So I sit in his chair, then I take the coin from under the papers. Sorry, Masta Chris . . . but you know how ma likes gold on her teeth. It was gonna be a present, see?'

'Well, they got it back,' Christopher said, sighing with relief. 'Put on the light, Jonah.'

'What for?'

Christopher grinned in the moonlight. 'Now that I'm no longer in mortal danger . . . I feel mortal hungry! Don't you?'

'You bet!' Jonah said, brightening. 'You stay in bed . . . I'll go hunting. I know just where ma hid some fried chicken – from me!'

Christopher was laughing when he reached up for Hippy Harry's charm, still dangling over his head. Then he threw the model of gallows and pirates right across the room.

By then Jonah had vanished.

Jonah believed in speed when the object was food.

From *Short Story International*

Oath of Friendship

Shang ya!
I want to be your friend
For ever and ever without break or decay.
When the hills are all flat
And the rivers are all dry,
When it lightens and thunders in winter,
When it rains and snows in summer,
When Heaven and Earth mingle —
Not till then will I part from you.

Anon, *Chinese, 1st Century BC (trans. Arthur Waley)*

Miss Smith and the Black Pearl

Maureen Lee

He danced his way to stardom – then came back to see his old teacher . . .

EXCITEMENT COURSED LIKE A FEVER THROUGH THE NARROW, century-old corridors of Penrose Road School on the day they heard James Ogori was coming back to see the end-of-term concert.

James Ogori was their inspiration, their ideal. He was living proof that even if you came from an area described as a 'sociologist's nightmare' such as Penrose Road, you could make it.

Success was not an impossible, worthless dream, but existed, waiting for anyone whether black, white, brown or yellow, if they worked hard and wanted it enough. Even if your Dad was out of work like Mr Ogori had been, or a dustman which Mr Ogori had eventually become, and you had a big brother always in trouble with the law. Despite all these tremendous hurdles and hazards, you could make it.

Like James Ogori had.

Of course, initially he owed it all to Miss Smith. He'd actually said that on television on more than one occasion when he was being interviewed.

There weren't any specialist teachers at Penrose Road School. Miss Smith was Class XI's Form Teacher and, painstakingly, she imparted the mysteries of spelling and sums and taught them how to draw and read stories. However, she took the whole school for musical movement and drama and it was then that Miss Smith came into her own.

In her black leotard covered in pulled threads and her laddered tights, she stood before the rows of children on the creaking boards of the hall, like a tiny beacon, back arched, arms outstretched, and willed, coaxed, cajoled, practically hypnotised them to dance.

And they responded. They flung their arms out like branches in a wind, kicked their legs, swung their hips and then, with eyes closed, forgot they would not be eating lunch and Mum wouldn't be home till eight o'clock that night when the factory shift finished or that Dad had clobbered them that morning for nothing in particular. They became lost in the lovely, languid movements.

What did it matter if they couldn't remember their three times table or thought cough ended with an 'f' and sometimes couldn't even understand what the teacher said to them.

They undulated, back and forth, in wonderful freedom to the music on Miss Smith's record player and pretended they were butterflies or gazelles or whatever she wanted them to be.

James Ogori was nine when he came to Penrose Road School and it was obvious straight away he was special. There was more zest in his movements, more rhythm in his steps, and on his face a look of ecstasy which told Miss Smith it wasn't just with his body he was dancing but with his mind and his heart too.

And what was so nice about Miss Smith was that she didn't shout at the rotten children, the ones with no sense of timing or two left feet, the ones who fell over. It was to them she was kindest.

'Very good, Helen,' she would say to a little girl who was too fat to touch her toes, or 'Nice movement, Bobby.' Bobby lacked coordination and couldn't remember which was left and right.

The better you were, the fiercer she became so everyone was happy really, because if she yelled, you knew you were good.

And did she yell at James Ogori!

'Bend!' she would screech, facing them, arms outstretched like a cross. Her brown-gray hair was cropped short, her skin had never known cosmetics and was waxy and colourless. But her eyes were bright, cornflower blue and they glared at James Ogori, willing him to do the impossible.

And sometimes it seemed he very nearly did, leaping to fantastic heights, taking unbelievable strides, all to please Miss Smith.

'You created me, you know that, Miss Smith,' he said once, his mischievous, chocolate eyes aglow and she replied crisply: 'Nonsense, child! God created you. Don't you listen in religious education?'

When he danced, bare from the waist up, he would glisten with oily perspiration and someone said he looked like a pearl. A Black Pearl. The name stuck.

Miss Smith had Mrs Ogori to the school and asked if James could possibly be sent to dancing lessons. Try as she could, what with four sons and a husband to support, Mrs Ogori couldn't think of a way she could raise an extra shilling, let alone the two pounds a week required – and they wanted a whole term in advance – so Miss Smith herself paid to send James to a good dancing school on Saturday mornings where at first the pretty girls and posh boys in their immaculate clothes and special shoes for this dancing and different shoes for that dancing, laughed at James Ogori in his shorts and bare feet.

But they didn't laugh when they saw him dance and as soon as Mr Ogori heard of this, and of how a chit of a white woman was paying out money on behalf of his son, he immediately took a job as a dustman. It was undoubtedly beneath his dignity to empty other people's rubbish, but to have your son partially supported by a lady who barely came up to your elbow was far more shameful.

Like everyone else, the Black Pearl had to leave Penrose Road School in July; he was eleven to go on to Comprehensive School. That was the year they did *West Side Story* for their end-of-term concert and James played the leader of the Puerto Rican gang.

You'd have thought it was a sort of 'thank you' to Miss Smith the way he did that part. He danced like magic, and the glittery dust of that magic touched the rest of the cast who felt as though a spell had been cast on them. They danced and sang like stars.

Mrs Ogori shed more than a few tears when she saw her son dance and sing so beautifully; her husband felt an unaccustomed lump of pride in his throat which refused to be swallowed and even the three older brothers, who'd been dragged there under the threat of an assortment of punishments, were impressed and regarded young James with respect forevermore.

Only Miss Smith appeared unimpressed and she calmly thanked the audience for coming and refused to let anybody take a bow by themselves.

The parents said she was a cool customer all right, but the children knew Miss Smith and could tell she was pleased with them. She didn't need words or looks to let them know how good they were.

There was never another end-of-term concert like *West Side Story*. That was special. Miss Smith went on with her musical movement classes and the children loved them just as much.

James did his five years at Comprehensive. Perhaps it was the dancing that gave him confidence his older brothers never had because he got six O levels and his dad pleaded with him to stay on. To have a lad at university seemed to Mr Ogori a pinnacle of parental success. Steadily, firmly, James refused.

Mrs Ogori went to see Miss Smith.

'He wants to go to London and on the stage,' she said, frightened for her baby.

James had never gone back to see Miss Smith, but she was not the slightest bit hurt. He would come one day, in his own good time, of that she was certain.

Now she answered Mrs Ogori, with the firmness and kindness she was loved for.

'He will never let you down. Let him go to London and the stage if that's what he wants. It's what he was born for.'

Inevitably James had been picked out of the chorus line of some second-rate show and given a solo part. Then he got a larger part in a better show, until at nineteen he'd been cast in the very same role in a revival of *West Side Story* that he'd played in Penrose Road School years ago. He was on his way to the top.

A famous songwriter had written a rock version of *Othello* specially for James Ogori and it was a tremendous success in London. Eventually, the show had gone to New York where James had been feted and adored and they'd made a film of it. Now everyone had heard of James Ogori and there was even talk of his being nominated for an Oscar.

Someone had resurrected the nickname and there he was on the cover of smart magazines and Sunday colour supplements, his black skin glistening like satin and 'The Black Pearl' brazened underneath while a dozen of his ex-classmates claimed to have thought of it.

Now, decided Miss Smith, he will come and see me. He's reached the very top of his career. Of course there is talk of more ambitious shows and films, but he will never be greater than he is today.

So it was no surprise when the headmaster told her one morning, 'I've had a letter from James Ogori – well, from his agent, in actual fact. He's coming back for the end-of-term concert.'

This year it was *Godspell* and Miss Smith told everyone that on no account must they be nervous because of James Ogori.

So they weren't because hadn't he once been there and sat at Anna Fuenzig's desk in top class and danced on that very same stage, and his father had emptied their dustbins; it meant they, too, might well come back as honored guests in ten years' time.

It was an adequate show. One of the girls had an exceptionally lovely voice, true and pure, so, you never knew! She might be as famous as Ogori one day. It was possible. Miss Smith had got her mother to arrange for real singing lessons.

James sat in front with his mother, who'd reached the point in late acquired wealth where she could leave her mink coat at home and not mention the swimming pool in the garden of her country home. Mr Ogori had come too, for sentimental reasons, and also one of the brothers who was James's manager and a good one at that. Another brother was in America writing songs of rare quality. But the oldest one? Well, there were a case of bad apples in many families.

After Miss Smith had thanked the children in her usual unemotional way, the headmaster came onto the stage and gestured to their guest to join them. Everyone cheered and clapped – they'd all heard so much about him. The children especially stared in awe.

James came onto the stage holding something glittery in his hands and he went up to Miss Smith and slipped it over her head. It was a fragile chain on which hung a delicate shell and, nestling inside it – a black pearl.

She stared down at the jewel without a word. She was grayer, more lined, perhaps because her beloved mother had recently died in great pain and the loss was hard to bear alone.

Her ex-pupil towered above her, slim and powerful in his tight jeans and black leather top, his skin gleaming like ebony. He held out his arms.

'They're going to dance!' someone murmured.

James moved her gently backwards and she whispered urgently, 'No!'

He looked startled. There'd been a note of near desperation in her voice.

'Miss Smith,' he said quietly so only she could hear, 'one of the ambitions of my life has been to dance with you. I was never good enough till now.'

James felt like a little boy again, back in her class, wanting her approval.

Miss Smith gave a rare smile, but it was tinged with anxiety. She didn't want to disillusion him, spoil things after all this time. But there was no alternative now. She had to tell him.

The audience was silent, wondering what was being said up there, wishing to be included.

'I can't dance, James,' she whispered hoarsely. 'I've got two left feet. I'm clumsy, Uncoordinated. Nothing's right. All I can do is make other people dance.'

She watched him worriedly, waiting for a frown and signs of disappointment. But James Ogori gave a gigantic grin and laughing, he picked Miss Smith up and carried her to the stage piano where he sat her, not too gently.

'I love you, Miss Smith,' he yelled to the world.

From *Short Story International*

The Black One

Charles Webster

His name was Karrupan, meaning the Black One, and he was the guardian of Ganesha's statue. A powerful tale from Sri Lanka.

IT WAS A PARTICULARLY UNPLEASANT STRETCH OF JUNGLE: CLOSE packed trees, soaking wet thorny undergrowth with leeches on almost every blade of grass. Apart from the leeches and an occasional monitor lizard, there seemed to be no wild life, if one ruled out a few fat green pigeons cooing and clattering their wings in the treetops.

I had missed my way, as I had done on previous occasions when on foot alone in the jungle. The faint game trail I had been following had petered out, leaving me stranded in this inhospitable tangle. Somewhere, whether in front or behind me I was not sure, was the small camp I had set up in an old *chena*, or clearing, in the jungle. Having no compass with me, I could not tell in which direction I was heading and the canopy of leaves overhead was too thick for me to get a proper sight of the sun. I was glad that I had provided myself with a cut lime on the end of a pointed stick with which to dab the leeches that swarmed up my boots. The acid in the lime caused them to curl up and drop off, squirming and frothing.

Hacking my way through the dense undergrowth, soaked to the skin, I eventually came out on to a narrow path that was not a game trail: a path that had obviously been made by human feet. I halted in surprise. Who would want to make a path in a place like this? It looked as though it was regularly used, twisting away through the trees, avoiding the clumps of thorny lantana scrub. Here there were few leeches and I decided to follow the path. Every road, lane or path leads somewhere, though by no means always where one wants to go. But to me, now, anywhere would be preferable to where I was. I sheathed the heavy knife I had been using to chop my way through the undergrowth and shouted loudly to warn anyone who might be about that I was coming. There was no answering shout.

The path twisted and turned like an agitated snake, skirting rocks, fallen trees and thorn scrub. After following it round in a semicircle, I saw what looked like ruins among the trees away to my right. This was a bigger surprise to me than the path had been. Ruins, here in this matted jungle? I had visited many of the Sri Lankan ruins, the so-called buried cities which had been painstakingly dug out of the jungle over many years, but I had not heard of any ruins in this particular part of the island.

I left the path and pushed my way through the bushes. There was little to be seen: some fallen columns carved with entwined figures, a stone pavement split by the roots of the trees, the remains of walls and a kind of bath, cracked and empty, carved out of a single large rock. The only thing that was more or less intact was a statue of Ganesha, the elephant headed Hindu God. It had the multiplicity of arms common to many Hindu gods, eight in this case. The top right hand held a string of beads, the second right hand a battle axe, the third hand offered protection and the fourth held one of the god's tusks. The top left arm had been broken off, the second left hand held a flower, the third a dish of sweetmeats and the fourth a snake.

I was studying the carving when I became aware that someone was watching me. I turned to see an old man leaning on a forked stick. He was very dark of skin, almost black, and wore only a dingy white loincloth. His face was as wrinkled as a dried walnut and his scant hair was done up in a small tight bun at the back of his head. He salaamed me gravely, his eyes searching mine. He was a Dravidian, a Tamil from South India. He addressed me in his native tongue, bidding me welcome. On my asking his name he told me it was Karrupan, meaning the Black One, adding that he was the guardian of the Ganesha's statue.

In the trees beyond the ruins I could see a small timber and thatch house. This was where he lived, Karrupan said. He had been a small holder on the fringe of the forest. When his wife had died five years ago, he had abandoned his piece of land and had wandered aimlessly in the jungle for some weeks before finding the ruins and the statue of Ganesha. Being a devotee of the elephant-headed God, he had decided to stay as guardian of the statue. There had been a village here a long time ago, he added, but the plague had come, wiping out the entire population. Abandoned and shunned by everyone the wooden and thatch houses, chewed to dust by termites, had collapsed. The jungle had moved in, felling Ganesha's little temple, leaving only the statue of the God intact except for the broken top left arm.

I asked Karrupan how he fared, what did he live on? He trapped pigeons and jungle fowl, he said, and there was an abandoned reservo   nearby which had supplied water to the village and which was the haunt of widgeon and teal and there were fish in it.

'And I watch the monkeys,' he added. 'What a monkey eats a man can eat.'

This may be true, but I would not care to eat some of the things I had seen monkeys eat, such as raw, live frogs.

'Does anyone ever come here?' I asked.

'No,' he replied. 'No one comes. They are afraid, They say the spirits of the dead are still here.'

'Then why don't you leave? There is nothing here for you All gods are just figments of the imagination, invented by man so that he could have something or someone to blame if things went wrong.'

He would not accept this.

'He is here,' he said, putting one hand on the statue's trunk 'If I look after him, he will look after me.'

'But it is a fever spot,' I protested. 'Mosquitoes will be breeding by the millions in that old reservoir.'

He swung his arm to point to a group of lime trees on the fringe of the ruins.

'If you eat plenty of limes,' he said, 'you will not get fever Mosquitoes do not like the lime juice in your blood.'

It was the first time I had heard this, but it could have been true. He showed no signs of being a malaria victim.

He invited me into his house for a meal. The meal was excellent – cotton teal roasted on a spit over an open fire, garnished with some edible roots. Though these looked rather revolting when cooked they tasted delicious. I complimented him on his cooking which seemed to please him. When we had finished eating, he asked why I was walking alone in the jungle.

'With no tracker. No *shikari*. It is not safe to walk in the jungle alone. There are many dangers.'

I explained that I had only started out for a short walk and had lost my way.

'But what about you?' I went on. 'You live on your own here. You walk alone in the jungle.'

'No, not alone,' he replied. 'I walk with Pellam Nai.' He pointed to a dark corner of the room and made a clicking sound with his tongue. A large dog rose out of the gloom and came towards him. Nearly as big as a mastiff, it had a rough coat and a tail like a long bottle brush. Its paws were huge and its eyes glowed menacingly in the firelight. It was well named Pellam Nai . . . a strong dog. Karrupan put his arm round the animal's neck.

'He will not hurt you,' he said, noticing my apprehension. 'His only enemies are the leopards and the jackals. When we walk in the jungle together, other creatures creep away into the undergrowth.'

'But what about snakes?' I asked.

Karrupan grinned.

'He can kill a cobra with one bite behind the head. He is as quick and brave as a mongoose.'

The dog came towards me and put his head on my knee. Tentatively, I put out my hand and stroked him and he thrashed the floor with his bottle brush tail.

'He has accepted you,' Karrupan said with evident pleasure. 'He will be your friend too now.'

I tried to find out more about this strange man and his self-imposed exile in this inhospitable place, but he would say little beyond what he had already told me. I thought of the early Christian hermits who had led just such lonely lives. He was as dedicated to his God as they had been to theirs. I glanced out of the door at the elephant headed monster on its pedestal. The third right hand offered protection. Karrupan had said the god would look after him. Knowing something of this particular Hindu deity who was worshipped as the God of wisdom, good luck, prudence and the remover of dangers, I concluded that Karrupan considered he was on to a good thing.

I went outside to inspect the ruins, though there was little that remained standing; the invading jungle had done its work well. It had been a small temple dedicated to Ganesha alone. I was joined by Karrupan and Pellam Nai. The dog sniffed among the fallen pillars and uprooted flag stones, but failed to find anything that interested him. There was little of interest to me either apart from the carvings on the pillars and the statue of Ganesha.

I remembered the story of how Ganesha had got his elephant's head. His mother, the Goddess Parvati, had gone swimming in the river and he had joined her in order to protect her from possible attack by bandits. His father, the God Shiva, riding by on his elephant, saw the pair frolicking in the water and, thinking evil, flew into a rage, drew his sword and smote off his son's head, which was carried away by the river. When he learned how innocent his son had been, Shiva was stricken with remorse, drew his sword again, decapitated his elephant and planted the severed head on Ganesha's shoulders, restoring him to grotesque life.

Telling Karrupan about my camp, I suggested he come back
ith me. I would give him a thing or two that would be of use
him, such as an axe or a hunting knife.

'How far is it?' he asked.

I gave him a rough estimate, about three miles.

'It is too far,' he said. 'I shall be outside Ganesha's
otection.'

'You will be quite safe with me,' I said, 'and you will have
llam Nai too. No harm will come to you.' I took him by the
m. 'Come, we will go now.'

Reluctantly, he agreed to go with me and we set off, following
e trail I had hacked through the jungle. Back tracking the
th, I found the place where I had gone astray. It was only a
w hundred yards from my camp in the old chena where my
ikari, Nayagam, would be waiting.

Coming out on to the game path I had followed originally,
e saw a large buffalo bull standing in the shade of a spreading-
ee. Pellam Nai, who had been following at Karrupan's heels,
ddenly took off and charged the buffalo, baying at the top of
s voice. Alarmed by this unusual behaviour on the animal's
rt, Karrupan shouted at him to come back. The dog took no
tice. It leapt, snarling, at the buffalo bull. The bull lowered
head and sent Pellam Nai flying with a sweep of its horns.
rrupan, brandishing his forked stick, stumbled in to save his
g. He failed to avoid the viciously swinging head. The point
one of the buffalo's great curving horns pierced his side just
low the rib cage, thrusting upwards.

Appalled by what I saw and remembering that I had told
rrupan that no harm would come to him, I snatched up a stout
len branch and rushed at the buffalo, yelling like a madman. A

hefty blow to the side of its head sent the beast staggering back t
turn and crash off, bellowing its rage, through the undergrowth
But the damage had been done. Karrupan lay crumpled an
gasping, blood flowing from the wound in his side. I cupped m
hands round my mouth and yelled for Nayagam, hoping he woul
hear me. I did what I could for Karrupan, but realised there wa
little or no chance of saving his life. By the time Nayagam cam
dashing breathlessly, the old man was dead.

'We must bury him here,' Nayagam said. 'The ground is sof
It will not be difficult.'

I shook my head.

'No. We will take him back to his house among the ruir
of the old temple.'

Together Nayagam and I cut bamboos and made a roug
stretcher. With Pellam Nai following at our heels, we carried th
dead man back to his house by the temple ruins. It was a har
exhausting journey with no protection against the swarmin
leeches. We laid him inside the little house and I filled th
interior with dry brushwood and set it alight. Karrupan woul
be cremated in the traditional Hindu manner, which I knew h
would have wished.

'What do we do with the dog?' Nayagam asked when the fi
had finally reduced everything to a heap of smoldering ashe
'Turn him loose in the forest?'

'No,' I said. 'He is not a young dog. He wouldn't survive
week in the jungle on his own. I will keep him.'

I knew Karrupan would have wished this too. I cut a length o
tough creeper for a lead and took the dog back to my camp.

He stayed with me on my plantation in the hills, guardir
me as he had guarded Karrupan, until he died a few month

later, old age having caught up with him. With Nayagam's help I made the long difficult trek back to the ruined temple and buried Pellam Nai at the foot of the statue of Ganesha. Two guardians for the spirit of Karrupan, the Black One.

Kafa, the Furious One

Peggy Albrecht

'When you go after a rogue elephant, it is either kill or be killed.'

IN MY COLLECTION OF IVORY ELEPHANTS, THERE IS AN UNUSUALLY beautiful one from West Africa. I call it Kafa. Delicately carved, highly polished, it stands on my desk, a paperweight too lovely to be placed on paper. Yet, this replica carved from the tusk of a rogue elephant is a constant reminder of a great tragedy.

As always, a feeling of thankfulness mingled with sorrow haunts me as I watch light and shadow dancing on the polished ivory. I'm thankful the gigantic Kafa, in whose image my miniature is carved, will suffer no more; thankful his raging is past, not future. Yet, sorrow overwhelms me for I cannot forget that one hour of terrible agony.

The nightmare began on a beautiful spring evening in 1975. A new moon hovered overhead and insects serenaded the peaceful village.

Inside the mission house, my husband, nursing a broken leg, was on the cot in the living room. I sat at the kitchen table helping our houseboy, Toma, with his English. He, in turn, was helping me polish my Mende.

Suddenly, our language studies were interrupted by a thump-hump and a deafening bellow behind the house. It sounded as though an angry monster had parachuted into our garden.

Toma rushed to investigate. He returned seconds later. His dark skin glistened with perspiration. His eyes bulged. He opened his mouth to speak but only a whispery gasp passed his lips. Finally, he was able to say, 'It is Kafa, the furious one. He is trampling cassava and uprooting banana trees.' Breathless from this speech, Toma turned and sped towards the village path.

'I must report,' he called over his shoulder. 'Kafa has the smell of palm wine.'

Fondness for the local palm wine had made the dusty white elephant notorious. Because he was the only albino of his kind in the country, he was easily recognised and his drunken antics were always laid to his account.

He had been in the area for over a year. It was thought that he had been attracted by a spectacular bush fire. He stayed on, evidently to enjoy the abundance of wine made by local tribesmen.

At first, he was harmless, an inquisitive, ravenously hungry clown. We enjoyed his escapades.

He consumed bushels of leaves, twigs, bark and coconuts along with gallons of liquid. His ever-sniffing snout not only led him to food and water, but to every well hidden wine barrel.

Once he had drained a barrel, he bellowed, rocked and rolled in drunken good humour. The rumblings of his stomach, the thump of his feet, and the slap-slap of his ears echoed far and wide. Yet, when he wished, he could move through the dense bush as quietly as a mouse.

The villagers were terrified by the silent movements as well as the uproarious rioting of this great white beast. Fearful and angry, they sent native hunters after him.

The pain inflicted by these hunters, whose guns were not powerful enough to kill, made him a rogue. Within a week he had tracked down two of his tormentors. He stamped them to a pulp, gaining for himself the name Kafa, the furious one.

From then on even the gardens he raided were completely destroyed – trampled in rage. The already short food supply was dwindling. Something had to be done.

We bought a 470 double barreled elephant rifle from a friend who was returning to the States. But by the time we secured a permit, Kafa had mysteriously moved on.

Now, he was back. We could hear the rumblings of his stomach above the thrashing of his feet as he moved into our neighbour's cassava patch.

Just as the sharp crackling of branches told us the old bull was destroying the neighbour's coffee tree, Toma returned. His hunter friend, Munda, muzzleloader in hand, was with him.

'Pa,' Toma said addressing my husband, 'Munda and I must kill Kafa.' He flicked his pink tongue across his lips.

'Tonight?'

'No, Pa, when the sky begins to gray.'

'You can't go after him with one muzzleloader. That would be suicide.'

'For true, Pa. Therefore, we are begging for your gun. Your big gun.'

"Toma. . . '

'I am able. You can remember I killed the crocodile with that gun.'

'Yes, but this is different. When you go after an elephant, it is either kill or be killed.'

'Pa, I know. I must hit him half-way between the eye and the ear.'

'Or on the forehead at the base of the trunk.'

'For true. I can aim for the bump if I meet him face to face.'

As they were talking, I felt my stomach tighten. I could not stand the thought of Toma facing this pain and wine crazed bull. Toma was young and tender-hearted. He loved all living creatures except snakes and crocodiles. He had no desire to be a hunter.

'Will you be able to shoot Kafa?' I asked. 'You say you pity the poor old creature.'

'I do, Mama. The hunters' bullets made him a rogue. It is not his fault. But he must die, because by now he is a dangerous adversary.'

'Aren't you afraid, Toma?'

'For the sake of fear my stomach is cold. But only Pa and I can use the big gun.' He shrugged his shoulders. 'My leg is not broken.'

The next morning, we were awakened before dawn by a tapping on our window. We heard Toma's tremulous voice saying, 'We go now.' With that they slipped away. By the time we reached the door, they were gone.

A dreadful hush hovered over the village all day. Only a few brave women went to the river to bathe and get water. None of the children went to the bush for firewood. The marketplace and the school remained empty. Most of the people sat in and around the barrier, speaking in hushed tones.

Then at 4:00 p.m. the stillness was shattered by a deafening scream and a furious thrashing in the bush. Moments later, a terrified Munda followed by Toma burst through the kitchen door.

'We done shoot 'em,' Munda gasped.

'He cannot agree to die,' Toma's breathless words were barely audible. His shoulders heaved. All at once his cheeks were wet with tears. He turned away to hide them.

'Where did you hit him?' my husband asked.

'We aim for the soft spot between his eye and . . .' Toma's voice broke. Munda continued the story.

'Then, Kafa moves like so,' he said demonstrating with a lift and turn of his head. Patting a spot to the left of his nose, he added, 'The shot striked here.'

'Near the base of the tusk?'

'For true, Pa.'

We groaned. There was no doubt in our minds the tormented tusker would soon come raging through the village that held the hunter's scent. Instead his terrified trumpeting and screaming subsided in the distance.

Within minutes, a noisy crowd of machete clutching villagers gathered in our compound. One man had a gun, fashioned from the steering column of an old jeep.

'They think the furious one is ready for death because he is now silent,' Toma said. 'They are calling for Munda and me to accompany them.' He started for the door. Clutching his stomach, he gagged as though about to vomit.

'His silence doesn't necessarily mean he is ready to die,' I warned. 'It may be a trick. You hit him in a nerve centre. He is more dangerous than ever.'

'You talk true, Mama,' Toma said turning his distressed face towards us. 'He is too clever. All day we track him. When we find his dung is not plenty warm, we think he is far ahead. Not so. He loops around to stand behind us. The poor creature has great pain, but he cannot forget his tricks.'

Neither Toma nor Munda wanted to go with such a large group, but the older men were insistent. At ten after five the party started down the bush path. Ninety minutes later, Munda returned alone.

From his hysterical report, we pieced the tragic story together. The party had followed the trail of blood and loose stringy dung to the Jong Swamp. There the gory evidence and the huge circular and oval prints of Kafa's fore and hind feet ended.

The older men hung head (consulted with each other) and decided the injured tusker had swum across. Immediately, they ordered Toma and Munda to lead the party around the swamp. Their attention was centred on the bush opposite the end of Kafa's trail. They had not gone six hundred feet when the great white rogue came crashing from the bush behind them.

With an enraged scream he tossed and crushed the panic stricken men as though they were made of straw. Toma and Munda fled to a giant baobab tree where Munda hid behind the massive trunk. Toma stood to one side. He aimed the 470 and prepared for Kafa's certain head-on attack. No doubt, he hoped to hit the orange-sized skull opening on his forehead.

But Kafa thundered toward him with head held high; his trunk curved like a giant fist. The first shot hit him in the chest. Then the mammoth tusker lowered his head and Toma fired the fatal shot, hitting the frontal bump. Kafa lunged, knocking Toma to the ground. A split-second later he toppled, crushing his courageous tormentor under his six tonne dead weight.

Though years have passed since that fateful evening, the sound of wailing echoes in my ears. I see again the faces of those who went to the Jong Swamp to recover parts of barely recognisable loved ones. I see and smell the carcass of the once mighty Kafa being mutilated by rats, roaches and driver ants.

Fortunately, I cannot picture Toma crushed beneath the stinking carcass. Instead, I see his handsome young face across the table. His eyes dance with amusement as he corrects my ridiculous pronunciation of a Mende word he knows so well.

I am thankful the nightmarish memories do not include the crushed body of this very special young man. If they did, I could not bear to keep the ivory Kafa on my desk. In that case, I would miss the exquisite reminder of Toma's friend, Munda. For it was the ex-hunter who carved my beautiful miniature and in doing so, discovered his real talent was carving – not killing.

Student Series, Short Story International

The Candidate who knew Too Much

Surendra Mohanty

'RIGHT, I'VE GONE THROUGH YOUR APPLICATION,' SAID PROFESSOR Klaus, without looking up at the candidate sitting across the table, 'Honestly, from what I see here, I'm not impressed. What makes you think you're fit for this post?'

Twenty-four-year old Albert was seeking the job of a teacher in physics at the Technische Akademie, Berne. He looked at Klaus, Professor of Physics, with little hope of getting selected. He had faced nine interviews in as many months, and had been rejected in each of them by men like Klaus.

'*Herr* professor, please don't go merely by those documents. Couldn't you give me an opportunity to demonstrate my abilities? Let me conduct a lecture, and you can judge for yourself. Any topic. . .' pleaded the candidate.

The professor's office was tastefully decorated with oak panelling covering the walls up to the door height. Above the panelling pictures of the world's greatest scientists hung – Galileo, Charles Darwin, Van Leeuwenhoek, Alfred Nobel, and the like – with their names and years of birth and death inscribed below. Behind the professor, hung a portrait of Newton, framed in carved mahogany, under which was written in bold SIR ISAAC NEWTON (1643–1727). There were also a few photographs that carried only the year of birth, the space after the hyphen was left blank. These were living scientists – Mendeleev, Wilhelm Roentgen and Marie Curie – yet the professor recognised their profound contribution and considered them worthy to be introduced into his gallery and his syllabus.

'Any topic! You've no experience, and your grades are nothing to speak of. Are you a *wunderkind* or what?' Mr Klaus raised his eyebrows briefly, without lifting his head, and glanced at him. He then lowered his eyes back to the file of papers on his desk.

These professors, they all look the same, thought the young man as he sized up Klaus. *Hair immaculately groomed, pale-eyed, with heavy spectacles. They always wear a perfectly starched and ironed shirt beneath a black jacket. And they seldom look at you directly through their glasses; instead they peer at you disapprovingly over the rim.*

'No, *mein* Herr. I didn't mean that. I just wanted to. . .'

'How come your school report isn't here?' interrupted Klaus with his next premeditated question. In fact, he had gone through his file meticulously, and was quite unnerved at what he found in it. He had prepared a volley of questions to snub the candidate at the interview.

'Well, actually, I didn't complete school. . . I mean, formally. Did it on my own. I am a trained teacher, done a four-year diploma in physics and mathematics.' He told the truth, as he always did, and, as on other occasions, saw the professor's jaw drop.

'You mean, you're a school dropout?' This time he looked straight through his glasses at the applicant, and noticed his ruffled hair.

'Well, I'm afraid, yes.'

Mr Klaus heaved a sigh, dropped his head to avoid further eye contact, and continued turning pages, 'Now, what's this picture doing in your file? Are you also trying for the post of art teacher?' he said with icy sarcasm. He made it appear spontaneous, though it was a well-rehearsed question from his arsenal.

'Oh no, Herr professor. That's the cover design of a research paper I'm working on. In fact, it's nearly complete. You'll find it in that booklet there.' The aspirant smiled, pleased that he finally got an opportunity to talk about his research work.

'It intrigues me; what research are you doing?' he continued questioning as he leafed through the neat handwritten booklet titled *Relativity*. The professor clenched his other fist under the table, in a bid to fight nervousness born out of jealousy.

The young applicant brightened up, moved forward in his seat and explained with enthusiasm. 'Let me explain. In my theory, I've expounded the relativity of time and space. The speed of light through vacuum -- and space is the ultimate vacuum -- is constant. Only relative motion can be measured. Since time and space are not absolute, but relative, even Newton's Laws of Motion are found inadequate.' He paused, quite satisfied with himself for having stirred the professor's intellect.

But it had quite the opposite effect. 'So you're going to teach me Newton's Laws of Motion? Or their fallacy? And according to you,' he tapped the thesis paper with his forefinger, 'all that we've learnt about Newton's Laws in the last hundred and fifty years are erroneous?'

'No, mein Herr. They are perfectly correct. Just some of his postulates suffer a drawback, when viewed. . . .' He sensed an agitation in the professor and thought it wise to speak no further.

'Yes? Why did you stop? Go ahead. Tell me, what else have you got here?'

Unwilling, but prodded, he went on, 'I've discovered the equivalence of energy and mass in an atom. You'll find it there on page fourteen. I've established a formula giving their relationship. My discovery remains to be proven experimentally, though. Energy equals mass multiplied by the square of. . .'

'Your discovery! Are you telling me you're some kind of a genius?' retorted Mr Klaus, in a burst of outrage. 'First you attempt to demolish Newton. Now some weird formula! Look, my dear. We have just stepped into the twentieth century; science no longer tolerates such nonsense.'

'Herr Klaus,' replied the young man resolutely, 'I didn't come here to be ridiculed. My theory has nothing to do with this job. Yet, if you are keen, I can explain it to you. Or else, I shall waste no more of your time.' He got up to leave.

'Mr Albert, let alone the position of a teacher, you're not even fit to be a technical assistant. Take your papers, and my advice – try your luck somewhere as a fiction writer.'

The candidate young Albert Einstein, left having been rejected for the tenth time, but, not, in the least, dejected. He was all the more determined to prove his mettle.

(The author teaches English at KiiT International School, Bhubaneswar)

Uncle Ken's Rumble in the Jungle

Ruskin Bond

UNCLE KEN DROVE GRANDFATHER'S OLD FIAT ALONG THE FOREST road at an incredible 30 mph. scattering pheasants, partridges and jungle fowl as he scattered along. He had come in search of the disappearing Red Jungle Fowl, and I could see why the bird had disappeared. Too many noisy human beings had invaded its habitat.

By the time we reached the forest rest house, one of the car doors had fallen off its hinges, and a large lantana bush had got entwined in the bumper.

'Never mind,' said Uncle Ken. 'It's all part of the adventure.'

The rest house had been reserved for Uncle Ken, thanks to grandfather's good relations with the forest department. But I was the only other person in the car. No one else would trust himself or herself to Uncle Ken's driving. He treated a car as though it were a low-flying aircraft having some difficulty in getting of the runway.

As we arrived at the rest house, a number of hens made a dash for safety.

'Look, jungle fowl!' exclaimed Uncle Ken.

'Domestic fowl,' I said, 'They must belong to the forest guards.'

I was right, of course. One of the hens was destined to be served up as chicken curry later that day. The jungle birds avoided the neighbourhood of the rest house, just in case they were mistaken for poultry and went into the cooking-pot.

Uncle Ken was all for starting his search right away, and after a brief interval during which we were served with tea and pakoras (prepared by the forest guard, who it turned out was also a good cook), we set off on foot into the jungle in search of the elusive Red Jungle Fowl.

'No tigers around here! are there?' asked Uncle Ken, just to be on the safe side.

'No tigers on this range,' said the guard, 'Just elephants.'

Uncle Ken wasn't afraid of elephants. He'd been for numerous elephants rides at the Lucknow zoo. He'd also seen Sabu in 'Elephant Boy'.

A small wooden bridge took us across a little river, and then we were in third jungle, following the forest guard who led us along a path that was frequently blocked by broken tree branches and pieces of bamboo.

'Why all these broken branches?' asked Uncle Ken.

'The elephants sir,' replied our guard, 'They passed through last night. They like certain leaves, as well as young bamboo shoots.'

We saw a number of spotted deer and several pheasants, but no Red jungle fowl.

That evening we sat out on the verandah of the rest house. All was silent except for the distant trumpeting of elephants. Then, from the stream, came the chanting of hundreds of frogs.

There were tenors and baritones, sopranos and contraltos, and occasionally a bass deep enough to have pleased the great Chaliapin. They sang duets and quartets from *La Boheme* and other Italian operas, drowsing out all other jungle sounds except for the occasional cry of a jackal doing his best to join in.

'We might as well sing too,' said Uncle Ken, and began singing the 'Indian Love Call' in his best Nelson Eddy manner.

The frogs fell silent, obviously awestruck; but instead of receiving an answering love-call, Uncle Ken was answered by even more strident jackal calls – not one, but several – with the result that all self-respecting denizens of the forest fled from the vicinity, and we saw no wildlife that night apart from a frightened rabbit that sped across the clearing and vanished into the darkness.

Early next morning we renewed our efforts to track down the Red Jungle Fowl, but it remained elusive. Returning to the rest house dusty and weary, Uncle Ken exclaimed: "There it – a Red Jungle Fowl!'

But it turned out to be the caretaker's cock-bird, a handsome fellow all red and gold, but not the jungle variety.

Disappointed, Uncle Ken decided to return to civilization. Another night in the rest house did not appeal to him. He had run out of songs to sing.

In any case, the weather had changed overnight and a light drizzle was falling as we started out. This had turned to a steady downpour by the time we reached the bridge across the

Suseva river. And standing in the middle of the bridge was an elephant.

He was a long tusker and he didn't look too friendly.

Uncle Ken blew his horn, and that was a mistake.

It was a strident, penetrating horn, highly effective on city roads but out of place in the forest.

The elephant took it as a challenge, and returned the blast of the horn with a shrill trumpeting of its own. It took a few steps forward. Uncle Ken put the car into reverse.

'Is there another way out of here?' he asked.

'There's a side road,' I said, recalling an earlier trip with grandfather, 'It will take us to the Kansrao railway station.'

'What ho!' cried Uncle Ken. 'To the station we go!'

And he turned the car and drove back until we came to the turning.

The narrow road was now a rushing torrent of rain water and all Uncle Ken's driving-skills were put to the test. He had on one occasion driven through a brick wall, so he knew all about obstacles; but they were usually stationary ones.

'More elephants,' I said, as two large pachyderms loomed out of the rain-drenched forest.

'Elephants to the right of us, elephants to the left of us!' chanted Uncle Ken, misquoting Tennyson's 'Charge of the Light Brigade,' 'Into the valley of death rode the six hundred!'

'There are now three of them,' I observed.

'Not my lucky number,' said Uncle Ken and pressed hard on the accelerator. We lurched forward, almost running over a terrified barking-deer.

'Is four your lucky number, Uncle Ken?'

'Why do you ask?'

'Well, there are now four of them behind us. And they are catching up quite fast!'

I see the station ahead,' cried Uncle Ken, as we drove into a clearing where a tiny railway station stood like a beacon of safety in the wilderness.

The car came to a grinding halt. We abandoned it and ran for the building.

The station-master saw our predicament, and beckoned to us to enter the station building, which was little more than a two-room shed and platform. He took us inside his tiny control room and shut the steel gate behind us.

'The elephants won't bother you here,' he said. 'But say goodbye to your car.'

We looked out of the window and were horrified to see Grandfather's Fiat overturned by one of the elephants, while another proceeded to trample it underfoot. The other elephants joined in the mayhem and soon the car was a flattened piece of junk.

'I'm station-master Abdul Ranf,' the station-master introduced himself. 'I know a good scrap-dealer in Doiwala. I'll give you his address.'

'But how do we get out of here?' asked Uncle Ken.

'Well, it's only an hour's walk to Doiwala, not with those elephants around. Stay and have a cup of tea. The Dehra Express will pass through shortly. It stops for a few minutes. And it's only half-an-hour to Dehra from here.' He punched out a couple of rail tickets, 'Here you are, my friends. Just two rupees each. The cheapest rail journey in India. And these tickets carry an insurance value of two lakh rupees each, should an accident befall you between here and Dehradun.'

Uncle Ken's eyes lit up.

'You mean, if one of us falls out of the train?' he asked.

'Out of the moving train,' clarified the station-master. 'There will be an enquiry, of course, some people try to fake an accident.'

But Uncle Ken decided against falling out of the train and making a fortune. He'd had enough excitement for the day. We got home safely enough, taking a pony-cart from Dehradun station to our house.

'Where's my car?' asked Grandfather, as we staggered up the verandah steps.

'It had a small accident,' said Uncle Ken. 'We left it outside the Kansrao railway station. I'll collect it later.'

'I'm starving,' I said. 'Haven't eaten since morning.'

'Well, come and have your dinner,' said granny. 'I've made something special for you. One of your grandfather's hunting friends sent us a jungle fowl. I've made a nice roast. Try it with apple sauce.'

Uncle Ken did not ask if the jungle fowl was red, grey, or technicoloured. He was first to the dining table.

Granny had anticipated this, and served me with a chicken leg, giving the other leg to grandfather.

'I rather fancy the breast myself,' she said, and this left Uncle Ken with a long and scrawny neck -- which was more than he deserved.